REVENGE IS BEST
SERVED HOT.

# THE WHITE WOLF'S WRATH

## SHEA HULSE

DRAGON FIRE AND DRUIDS BOOK ONE

# THE WHITE WOLF'S WRATH

## SHEA HULSE

HOT TREE PUBLISHING

# THE WHITE WOLF'S WRATH

## DRAGON FIRE AND DRUIDS
### BOOK ONE

SHEA HULSE

HOT TREE PUBLISHING

For information, contact the publisher, Hot Tree Publishing.

WWW.HOTTREEPUBLISHING.COM

EDITING: HOT TREE EDITING

COVER DESIGNER: BOOKSMITH DESIGN

E-BOOK ISBN: 978-1-923252-02-8

PAPERBACK ISBN: 978-1-923252-03-5

*For my family, both the given and the chosen.*

# PROLOGUE

ONE WOULD IMAGINE THE WORST DAY OF MY LIFE WOULD be remarkable in some way. But the day I became an orphan was like any other. I remember it was mild, a good day for breaking midwinter blues, and the women were tidying up, dusting here, organizing there. Though really, we had all been living under the strain of what was coming and occupying ourselves with trivial matters instead to keep our minds off it. As we had been for a while now, making the days bleed into nights under the weight of the unknown.

The stress began the night it was announced that I was betrothed to Oisin, a worthy match for a woman of my station. We had a significant manse near Carrick-on-Shannon in county Leitrim; my father, the lord of our clan, made his wealth dealing in precious gems. On that night, a feast was held, the revelry was palpable, and gossip flowed as swiftly as the wine.

That was the first I'd heard of the war, though then it was perhaps only a few skirmishes. Men from the north of us, wild and unruly, causing mayhem farther south. Women gasped, and men plotted, shoring up their defenses, making allegiances where they might prove necessary.

The news wasn't unheard of or even noteworthy at first. We were battle-hardened people. My father wasn't lord by lineage, though that was often the way—as it was the way I would claim the right to rule upon his death. A death that happened far sooner than anyone could have foreseen. Though, how many could say the same? It wasn't as if anyone could tell us what tomorrow would bring.

No, my father won this land with his fists and his wits. Venturing north as a young man, he whetted his blade on the unruly clans that had occupied our land before us, making a name for himself. Perhaps that was why they came south now, seeking retribution. Particularly on the eve of the kingdom my father sought to establish with my marriage to Oisin.

But I sat silent as a lodestone grew in my belly, causing a feeling of unease like I had never known.

The girls in my group teased that it was only marriage jitters, but I was no stranger to men, and certainly not to Oisin, whom I'd played and laughed with since childhood. No, I was content to marry him. He was a fine gentleman, and his family was well established in their own clan, his father a lord there as well. Our combined wealth once we wed would be far superior to any clan near us, ensuring our hold on the land that would also double in size.

No, the feeling that plagued me was other-worldly, an emotion without a name. It was like the hairs that rose on the back of your neck or the feeling of being watched, something primitive and feral.

So while they danced, I sat primly, the lady of the house—or queen, as I would be after our parents' reign once the challengers were success-fully thwarted. That thought brought with it some alarm. And in that chair, I watched keenly for the disturbance, for what made my heart sit in my throat and my belly twist in knots. But I saw nothing for once, no flicker of a flame gone awry, no furtive glances from the guests, not even a dog acting strangely to show me why I felt so heavy.

The women kept their chattering going, and I nodded and smiled as I ought to, and few, if any, of them saw my unease. I couldn't hide from Evelyn, though. The housekeeper caught my eye more than once, a question and an answer.

She felt it too.

But for the good of the clan, we would remain neutral for now—until I got any sign of true danger, at least. A glance toward my parents confirmed their suspicions as well, but the stern look said to hold strong. Nothing was amiss until something happened.

Only, what was to happen?

I had questioned my parents later, both tight-lipped and eyes crinkled with concern. While my mother tried to soothe my fears, wringing her hands and smoothing my hair back, my father lectured me on my training and keeping watch over my mother.

Though not a frail woman, my mother was not as hearty as me or my father. What she lacked in stature, she made up with a strength of character that lent her an air of intimidation. Though neither of us measured up to my father. His barrel chest and furrowed brow commanded attention everywhere he went. Behind his measured gaze, I knew he was fair and kind, so long as you respected him and others.

I'd only seen a few men beheaded by his hand, but none I could say that were done without due cause. And fewer still crossed him the more times he was forced to swing the death blow—save me. I had a knack for turning his complexion ruddy in frustration, but I was the exception to the rule, and we all knew it.

That was three nights ago, and the weight bore down more heavily as we swept the dirt and shined the windows. The wedding was to happen in four days' time. Winter weddings were less common, but Oisin's family made their legacy on their livestock, and spring brought calving season.

While we worked, I thought about the talk I'd heard about the Raiders. My family never held to traditional roles, refusing to make someone do for them what they wouldn't also do themselves, something I had admired, as had our clansmen. The work was simple and monotonous, but it made me appreciate our lot in life, which I think was a second reason behind working alongside the men, women, and children we were in charge of. It brought it home, making their problems ours as well.

The frequency of the reports and the devastation had only increased, and talk of war was more prevalent. I had tried to speak to my parents about my intuition, but they asked me to think only of the wedding, that it was more important. I could hardly see how that was possible, but even Evelyn had been tight-lipped about it.

The girls rarely contributed much to my anxieties. There were only four of us—myself and three other highborn girls from the clan—but often, despite the friendships, I felt alone. Cara and Fallon were sisters, both effervescent and prone to giggling, and Erin was more astute and proper than I would ever want to be. If anyone ought to be queen, it would be her with her primness.

While the sisters would scoff and talk of how Oisin might look naked and of how lucky I was to marry such a good-looking and wealthy man, Erin would chide me for childish sensitivities. Then she would proceed to politely excuse herself from the other girls' indecent discussions.

While I cleaned, I swept up a massive black feather, somehow unnoticed before. I froze in place, the raven's caw echoing ominously in the distance as if on purpose. Too coincidental to be accidental.

The clamor began next, before the horn sounded —once to open the gates, twice to close them, thrice to prepare for battle. Like a swarm of bees, the sound was palpable as much as audible. A sudden tension filled the air, followed by murmurs, before the first blast broke the peaceful sunny day. At first no one moved, all frozen in whatever state they had been in. Women hunched over washbasins, men froze with their horses, even children stopped their games in anticipation.

The third and final echoing blast that followed was hardly unexpected for me—it was the answer I had been anticipating—whereas for others, it unleashed a flurry of activity. Most women ran to hide, their washing left behind. Some hurried to their children and families, while I went toward the clash of metal, the broom forgotten.

Running to the armory, I emerged wielding a sword from my father's collection, brushing past women and children in their flight. The dagger at my side was inadequate for true bloodshed, and I was too short to want to get close to any enemies with the small knife when they would likely have a broadsword. Before long, I reached the back lines of the men protecting our gates just as the front lines had broken.

It was too fast. I'd hardly had time to grab a weapon before men were running in the opposite direction. How were we broken so swiftly? So easily?

That was when I saw the banners. A wolf's head on a black background, howling at the moon. The White Wolf, a man of myth and mystery. Suddenly, our swift defeat made more sense.

Men scattered, some to reform and others for the hills. I'd held my ground, losing it little by little until my back was to the rear yard.

Giants stood before me, ten feet tall at least, swinging weapons as large as tree trunks like they were feather dusters. Men fell in swaths beneath their clubs and swords and axes, proving why we had failed so miserably.

That was when I saw them. In the melee after the lines had broken, behind the massive ogres, the dragons soared low and viciously, riding the wind like hawks—only a handful of them. They were beautiful, savage things, an array of colors blending perfectly with the scenery.

Heat scorched and fires erupted as the winged devils attacked ruthlessly. Though I couldn't focus on them long if I wanted to keep my head, I thought

I saw men on their backs before steel flashed in my vision, bringing my attention back to my surroundings.

I didn't know how many men I cut down, or whether I truly had or not. More had ignored me than engaged with me, and the few who did were lost in the mess that was my home.

I'd failed to best the last man who swung my way; my only memory was pain and falling before the world disappeared. When I came to, it was through one eye that I looked around at my surroundings, the other swollen shut. Chestnut hair caught my attention, followed by a familiar dress, and my heart leaped into my throat.

Blinded for another reason entirely, I screamed when I saw her face. The sweetest one I had ever seen, pale and frozen in death. A gash ran across her chest, red smeared the front of the dress she loved so much, and more seeped into the ground beneath her body. My mother looked peaceful even now, despite the horror of her demise.

I was not so peaceful.

It must have been a while since I'd been knocked out, the twilight bleeding into the brilliant blue sky like the men who bled into the earth now. Lights blazed through the windows of my manse. Men's shadows could be seen through the curtains, reveling in their victory.

Blind rage sent me careening toward my house, wobbly with a vicious blow to the head. I grabbed my sword and stormed through the kitchen door, hell-bent on revenge.

Only to be stopped by the cook.

There wasn't a kinder soul than Evelyn, so much so that with a gentle nature and fresh biscuits, she had won the hearts of the vagabonds. Likely the latter had won them over, proving her value.

Her biscuits could win wars.

But her exclamation of "Sarah!" stopped me in my tracks as she pulled me by the hand to the sink.

She didn't speak as she stashed the sword under the wooden worktable in the center of the massive kitchen. There were sacks of all kinds sitting off the floor on wooden slats under the table. She silently slid it out of sight beneath them, blood and all.

Cornering me by the basin, she held me there as she wrung a cloth in the water before facing me again. Wiping with gentle efficiency, she cleaned the blood off me, tears shining in her brown eyes.

Adrenaline still pumped through my veins like a hurricane, and my breathing was as shallow as a puddle, but one shake of her head had me taking a deep breath. *Not here, not now,* it seemed to say.

When she looked at me pointedly, stopping her cleansing, I knew she was telling me to bide my time. I shook my head, clenching my teeth.

"Oisin lives," she dared whisper so quietly, I squinted as if that would make me hear better.

Words failed me, but the shock on my face must have registered, as she continued.

"Paddy was here. He tells me he's hurt but alive."

Paddy was the stable master and farmhand who had fought alongside me. I didn't imagine anyone could have survived, and relief swept through me at the few who remained. Followed by devastation at those who had not.

"How?"

"Michael. He is with him now. And I need you to be with me now, do you understand?"

I nodded, adrenaline ebbing away into a cold resolve. Evelyn needed me, and I would not fail her. Just as Michael, Paddy's son, would care for Oisin. He was employed by the king's family and must have come to check on his father in the aftermath.

"Where?"

But she shook her head. With an invading army, Oisin was a wanted man now and too valuable to our clan to risk saying too much. Though it killed me not to know where or how he was, I let hope keep me from doing anything hasty.

I was worth more alive than dead right now too. I could bide my time until then. Besides, who else would protect Evelyn? Paddy was close but not close enough; this way, I could watch her and await my soon-to-be husband's recovery.

Oisin was alive.

The knowledge was dangerous. If anyone knew the would-be king and queen remained, we would be routed out and beheaded instantly. We were a threat to the invaders, who had indeed come to claim our wealth for themselves. But we wouldn't be so easily dispatched, it seemed.

My betrothed was valiant, what a prince ought to be. Tall and lean, his dark hair and eyes pleasantly offset his porcelain skin. The Beirne clan was well established for generations, but clans far more stable and respected had fallen to the banners emblazoned with the White Wolf's head snarling in defiance.

Oisin, my friend since childhood, when we would chase each other through the fields with the other children of nobility. There were only a few in our clan, but enough of them that rank mattered. I hadn't grown to know him more intimately until our betrothal.

We were to be married in a few days. My family being the most prominent noble house with a daughter of marriageable age made us a perfect match.

Throughout our teen years, I would see him at functions to chat about whatever drivel was acceptable in polite society. I hadn't been interested in marriage then, though we might have married much sooner if I had been. My father had always listened to my opinions.

"Listen, child," Evelyn said, a disheartening way to start. "The men are in the house now. Heaven knows why they're here, but I need you to be quiet and bide your time. Do you understand me, *Sarah*?"

I nodded, words beyond my ability at the moment.

"You'll cook and clean with me, and we'll make do until we know more, okay, sweetheart?"

I moved my head again, a strangled sound escaping my lips.

"My m-m...," I began, trying to convey the devastating scene that I had found on the lawn only minutes before.

"I saw. I'd thought you had joined her, but the gods smiled on you today. Let's keep it that way."

"Father?" I choked out.

"I don't know, but we'll find out one way or the other."

Evelyn had called me Sarah Burke after a famous dramatic actress, a popular moniker from my childhood when I was a wild toddler prone to pouting if I didn't get my way. It worked, since I was already used to answering it.

And a far cry from my actual name, Emer. Emer Flynn was now a ghost, and with her went my long, curly brown hair. As we stood there, sequestered by the basin, Evelyn took the kitchen scissors to it after cleaning the blood off me, luckily in peace.

That was when I cried.

I cried over my shorn hair, once long, thick, and wavy, now a bob barely touching my chin. She had slowed down then, taking the length in front of my face before clipping it with scissors to give me bangs.

Before the tears had stopped, she'd taken my bundle of hair and shoved it up my skirts, wrapped in her apron. She tucked my hair into my corset strings with one hand and ripped my underskirt off with the other. Fashioning an apron out of my skirts to hide the blood, she finally stepped back and wiped my tears.

I had reeled it in then, though I could have cried for hours. But the time for crying was later. Right now, I needed to blend in.

She'd directed me to the bathroom to gather myself. Standing in the small room, I washed the remaining blood off my hands, then scrubbed at the splotches on my dress furiously, a fit of mania ensuing over the bloodstains. My breathing hitched, and I deflated, withering like a fire without air. Staring at the reflection in front of me, I examined the damage.

Not only was my eye red and swollen, purple veins exploding behind my skin and crisscrossing like lightning in the night sky, but I also had a split lip and multiple bruises. My hair was gone, the luxurious oak brown, so like my mother's, short with the look of a fresh cut, rounder and sharper at the same time.

Frankly, it looked flattering. The bangs framed my dark lashes, making me look exotic and feral, and the bob accentuated my broad shoulders, making my otherwise muscular body shapelier.

But it was another battle lost, another name to mourn.

GRIEVING WAS SOMETHING I DID OFTEN NOW. UNTIL nights turned into days, and the other way around, until I didn't know which was which anymore, much less care about the distinction. They were all one lump of emptiness and sorrow, interjected with Evelyn as she floated in and out of my consciousness. I was never sure if I was awake or dreaming, nor did it matter really.

Only Oisin mattered now.

The attack had been a few weeks ago—weeks without news of Oisin. The purple of my eye turned grotesque and yellowed with the fading injury. Then one day my vision returned, sometime after the swelling had disappeared.

Evelyn was relieved by that. I couldn't say I noticed either way.

Men came and went through the kitchen and the manor, doors opening and shutting, conversations both loud and quiet, all in snippets of awareness amid the indifference that kept its grip on my existence. The winter days flew by and moved slower than molasses as I gradually took on more chores and failed at many of them.

I would have been queen; instead, I was scrubbing pots in the kitchen—a task my staff used to do for me.

It wasn't that I couldn't wash dishes or do a plethora of other things my status didn't require. There was just so much loss. The kind that made getting out of bed feel useless, food taste like sawdust, and my bones ache. If it weren't for Oisin, I wouldn't have continued.

But he was alive, if gravely wounded. I didn't know his family's welfare, but if I had to guess, the chances weren't great. So I had to carry on; if mine was the last friendly face he saw, it was my duty to provide it.

In the weeks of our courtship, I found the adult Oisin to be soft-spoken but highly intelligent, not unlike his child self I had known. He was kind and considerate, gentlemanly. I couldn't say whether I was in love with him yet, but he had proven he would be a wonderful husband.

At the least, I was smitten. And I was determined to honor our parents and do right by Oisin. So, I would fight for our freedom and future while he couldn't.

I'd have fought to prevent this if I could have. I hadn't seen the battle, though that's not to say I didn't see anything.

My mother couldn't fight; my father had reminded me to stay with her. She needed me more.

She did need me, and I'd failed her.

Besides, I was no match for the White Wolf or his entourage. I'd have been cut down before I could even see one of those dragons that accompanied him.

Not only dragons but Fae, giants, and fantastic beasts I had no vocabulary to name. The battle had been merely a formality. Our clan didn't want to give in without a fight, but it was clear from the banner that waved above the approaching army that we were outmatched.

Outmatched, outnumbered, and outstrategized. The shield wall they had used was far superior to ours, covering their shins, bodies, and heads. And after luring us into the valley, they closed ranks behind us with a force that had hidden in the woods.

We would have been slaughtered where we stood if we hadn't surrendered. Choking off our escape route also let the hooligans through to our manor, where I unsuccessfully tried to save my home.

I only hoped I wasn't recognized, neither by the men I had battled nor by any of the prominent men who now prowled the halls where I had grown up. Heaven knew what they would do with me now as a maid, much less a noblewoman. Some men would keep me as their prize if only they knew.

My face wasn't one to be forgotten, not among the nobility. Not for looks, though my thick, long lashes were striking against my fair skin. No, my brown eyes and hair were lovely, but the power my family wielded was unforgettable.

*Had* wielded. The word made my eyes burn.

No wonder the manor home was immediately targeted, nor was it a wonder that the White Wolf himself took it as his residence. My father had been a kingmaker in his own right, a jeweler of the finest quality; his coffers ran deep. Our home was bedecked in luxuries from worlds away, sparing no expense on our comfort.

As the only daughter of a wealthy family, I was hard not to notice, especially when my throat was worth more than most people made in a lifetime because of the cost of jewels that graced it. Most men cared only for that, though—particularly these sorts of men. So I hoped I could remain anonymous and that no one had seen me at any functions before. Not that they would find any jewels on me now, or likely at all. Being our main source of income, we had hidden them in the preparation for war.

Not that there could be a ransom for me anymore. No one but Oisin cared. And Evelyn, but she wouldn't have any money to spare on me. But this kind of man could be cruel to women, no matter their status.

I was better off being invisible.

CHAPTER
# ONE

There hadn't been dragons in existence for centuries.

And I wasn't always a traitor.

But that all changed when the White Wolf came down from the north, bearing down on us with an army unlike any we had seen before.

Nothing was ever the same again.

I'd been a lord's daughter then, betrothed to the heir to the throne. Now, I was an orphan, my fiancé suffering from wounds he'd received in the battle for our freedom.

And I was a servant to the man responsible for my despair.

I was a prisoner in my own home—my old home—because now it belonged to my enemy, as did I.

The White Wolf, Whalen Walsh of the Dartry Mountains, was a name told to children when they misbehaved. I had heard it when I was a girl and he was still the young wolf, his namesake.

We weren't as young as we had been, but I was astonished at how young the infamous vagrant was when I first laid eyes on him. I had expected a man past his prime with a weathered face and gray hair.

How else would he have amassed such a reputation?

But the man who now slept in my parents' bedroom couldn't have been more than thirty, close to my fiancé's age. That was perhaps all they had in common, though.

Oisin was a fine warrior, but his primary occupation was as the prince of our territory. He'd spent much of his time reading about war strategies rather than engaging in actual war, until Whalen came down with his dragons and war was upon us.

Whalen was war incarnate, with hair and eyes as wild and untamed as a battle. But the latter was what sent a shiver down your spine.

You knew you were prey and he was the predator when you looked into his eyes. Like twin icicles, the blue was nearly white, equally cold, and emotionless.

How he sized you up in a glance and discounted you as inferior made you clench your teeth. But you couldn't do anything if you wanted to live.

His long hair was like a wheat field stained red with blood. Perhaps it was. The strawberry color of his hair was lighter than the red of his short beard that added to its mass.

If he bathed during the evening, he left it unbound to let the tresses dry. So many thick curls shouldn't belong to a man with his reputation.

Though if the locks didn't match it, his shoulders did. Sticking out from beneath his mane like mountain peaks, they were brutal and relentless enough to incite fear.

He had a woman with him who braided his hair intricately, a beautiful blonde who looked nearly as wild as him. There was an intimacy between them that made me think they were together. With his hair pulled back, you could see the full might of him that the furs he wore couldn't hide.

He was massive—all lean muscle, but a lot of it —twice the size of any man I had met before. His biceps were as large as my head, his hands as big as bear paws; he towered over the other men by head and shoulders, dwarfing them.

When you were close to him, you understood

how he had gained his reputation. And he'd done that before he had dragons in his entourage.

Some rumors were ostentatious, like eating his enemies and making a throne of their bones. Others were previously thought to be impossible but now held a note of truth, like having giant's blood or wrestling a bear barehanded and winning. Before, giants weren't real, and no one was the size of a bear. Now, I couldn't say that either of those things was false.

The one rumor that remained questionable was that he wasn't only deemed the White Wolf due to his name or his furs. That he would change shape like the tales we'd been told as children—men who could alternate between human and animal at will, a valuable ability in times of war that seemed to crop up in darker times.

Perhaps it was just a way to explain the ferocity of a warrior so adept at their trade that it seemed they were something more than human. Or a way to embolden frightened soldiers facing the opposition. Maybe even to frighten the enemy.

But that was before the other rumors proved true.

No one knew where the supernatural creatures came from or how they existed after so many years.

My father had mumbled about a powerful witch and her dragon, oral histories he'd received from his elders and theirs before them in the form of stories told half in his cups around the fireplace. Legends of the magically gifted had been passed on for generations, but no human who lived now had ever seen them before Whalen came marching them south.

To what end needed to be clarified. Our story was very similar to the others: When the White Wolf came marching, you had no choice but to yield. He would stay only long enough to recoup before continuing. A force of nature, he would chew you up, spit you out, and leave you reeling, never the same again.

At least *I* would never be the same again.

So I did the only task I could competently do: wash the dishes. Bowls and utensils were piled on the counter, and I set to them as Evelyn prepared dinner.

That was the most grating part of the ordeal after my hair.

Strangers could sleep in our beds. We'd had strange guests before.

But it was galling that they would eat our food, too, when my parents were gone and would no longer eat. Evelyn would prepare an undoubtedly delicious meal for these mongrels while my family and loved ones went without.

Not that they knew the difference anymore. Except for Oisin.

Oisin was the beat of a drum, the pounding of my blood; every pump went *Oisin, Oisin, Oisin*. I branded his image in my mind—his fair skin, his chocolate hair, his midnight eyes. The way his voice was gentle and smooth, like honey and tea, with enough sharpness to make it masculine.

Every dish I washed, every pot I scrubbed, I chanted, *Oisin*. I said it when I had no appetite and Evelyn forced me to choke down bread and broth. I prayed for him at night on a threadbare blanket on the floor in Evelyn's room, a level below my lavish bedroom.

And now, as I scrubbed a stubborn pot, I said his name as one of the men who had taken over my home and my land scoured the kitchen, complaining that Evelyn was shorting them of meat. They tore through the kitchen prior to raiding the cellar, then returning.

Outside the window beyond the sink, a bird called out, flapping its wings in its retreat. I didn't need the warning to know trouble was brewing, but I thanked the spirits anyway. The hair rose on the back of my neck as I tuned in to the conversation behind me.

"What is this?" their leader said, slamming a slab of cured ham onto the table.

He was a short man with small black eyes and a bald head. When they made their way to the cellar, I had peeked to confirm he was one of the men I had battled.

He had entangled with me before a blow knocked me down, and he continued past me while I engaged the next person who came running up. It seemed as if he'd run away so he didn't have to deal with me.

Men like him were weak; they made up for their smallness by trying to dominate those around them. They deemed themselves gods among men so they could feel better about their inadequacy, but they convinced only themselves.

I kept my back to him for fear of exposure as the smell of the ham permeated the air. His other two companions flanked the kitchen, all masculine male idleness itching for a fight.

"Ham, sir," Evelyn stated matter-of-factly.

I had to bite my lips to stop the laugh that threatened to bubble past them. That asked for more trouble than I wanted, but so had Evelyn's response.

"Don't act smart with me, woman. I know what ham is. I'm asking why, if you have all this meat, you are not feeding it to us."

"Are you planning on acquiring more, sir?"

"Am I planning on getting more? Why, so you could steal more for yourself instead of feeding us?"

His anger made him stupider as he stalked closer to Evelyn to put his ugly mug in her face. Sweet Evelyn, with her delicate white hair and striking hazel eyes, was a kind soul but not a pushover. I peeked as she stood to her full height, half a head over the short man, her rounded figure straightening at the insult.

"Why, sir? I don't eat meat; I have no taste for it. I only ask because when you finish this ham, that's the last of the meat, and I know how you boys enjoy it so," she finished, her voice oozing with sarcasm.

And she called me dramatic.

The man didn't miss the intended insult as he raised a fist to strike her. I didn't remember moving, but the chef's knife in the sink, waiting to be washed, was in my hand suddenly and pressed against the man's throat faster than I thought possible.

I couldn't recall grabbing it, but there it was, coated in water and soap as my hand was, traveling down my arm to splat loudly in the echoing silence that followed.

I maneuvered my back to the sink to watch both of the other men lest I be stuck in the back with a knife myself. The man in my arms floundered like an idiot, a fish out of water, but I pressed the knife harder against his throat until he stood still.

The water made it hard to grip the knife, but I asked for strength and found a stronger position. Clarity swept through me, replacing the cobwebs with a deadly sharpness that brought every instinct to life.

"Were you about to hit my lovely cook here, sir?" I growled the last word so he knew what I thought about him.

More flailing around, trying to strong-arm out of my grip. But I knew Evelyn, and her knives were never dull. When I pressed the edge just so, his sharp intake of breath sounded as blood welled up beneath the blade.

"Did you not hear me? I asked you a question. Are you harassing this poor woman you see in front of you?"

The miserable worm finally nodded his affirmative, too spineless to mutter the word. His pals looked peeved but unwilling to help. That was the trouble with men like this: Put their back against the wall, and their cowardice took over. They would lie, cheat, and steal to survive for what they wanted.

It made them weak and unpredictable, which also made them a liability.

I was preparing to launch into a diatribe about his manhood when the kitchen door swung open to reveal the White Wolf himself, his thick furs secure around his massive shoulders, making him larger than life. His eyes locked on mine, and I felt the full force of his dominance in them, but I wouldn't balk. He smiled then, and the look was nothing short of predatory.

"I thought I smelled blood," he said by way of explanation. His deep voice was smoky, smooth, rich, and fiery.

"Aye, you'll smell more of it if you don't keep your men in line," I snapped.

I didn't know if his look was one of approval or if he was about to disembowel me, but I was drawing a line in the sand. Even if it got us both killed, I'd rather die on my terms than live on theirs. I could be their slave for Evelyn and Oisin, but I wouldn't tolerate any abuse, not even for Evelyn.

"And how do you suppose I do that, miss...?"

"Sarah," I replied, quickly supplying the fake name. "And I would kill this one immediately; he's not worth the trouble he brings."

He waved a hand in a go-ahead gesture, never breaking eye contact with me. So I did.

I gripped the man's hair with my free hand and slid the edge across his throat, cutting off his pleas for help swiftly. As I let him slump to the ground, moments from his last breath, I squared my shoulders again.

"I'll cook and clean, but I'll not tolerate disrespect. We will be treated honorably," I stated with as much authority as I could invoke.

"Is that so?" Walsh said, looking at me intently.

My heart pounded so viciously in my chest that I thought he could see it through my clothes. Breath was hard to come by, and the shallow pants I managed rasped through my lungs like broken glass.

He let the seconds tick ominously by, holding me in his predatory gaze. If I wasn't mistaken, he may have smiled, a wicked thing filled with promise.

A promise of what, I didn't know. I wasn't altogether excited to find out, though.

"So it is, then," he continued, addressing the men still standing there, gaping at their fallen acquaintance. "There will be no tolerance for incivility to the ladies or any of the others here," he amended, looking to me for acceptance.

I nodded my gratefulness.

"Do you understand?"

They both mumbled, "Aye, sir," with bowed heads. Their fists were clenched in outrage, but they knew better than to say anything now.

"Now, take MacGowan out and bring him around to the front steps so everyone knows what will happen if they don't treat our friends here with care."

"Aye, sir," they parroted again.

"Then come back here and clean up the blood and return the meat to the cellar."

More ayes, and with a wave of his hand, they were dismissed. They got to work immediately, taking the hands and feet of their fallen comrade and carrying him out the back door.

I was glad for the body to be gone. Though the blood threatened to make me ill, I wouldn't show that to Walsh.

"Is this truly the last of the meat?" he asked, addressing Evelyn.

*Was he listening?* I thought idly. A faraway place

in my mind wondered how he was so aware of the scuffle we had been having.

"Yes, sir," she said, and I was proud of her unwavering voice, her shoulders still squared.

"I'll send a hunting party out. Is there anything else that you need, miss?"

"Mrs. Connelly—Evelyn, if you like. I'll make a list, sir, if that would suit you."

"Thank you, Evelyn. When you've finished, you can bring it to me or have Sarah bring it. I imagine by tomorrow?"

"Yes, sir."

"Perfect," he said, his hard eyes masking any indication of the thoughts behind them. "Anything else you need, don't hesitate to bring it to my sister or me; I'm sure you've seen her with me before."

"Yes, sir."

"You may call me Whalen if it pleases you, Evelyn, Sarah." He turned his head to address me as well. "My apologies that we haven't had the chance to meet formally."

"It's quite all right, sir. You are busy."

"I should never be too busy to acknowledge the hand that feeds me—and quite successfully at that," he said, pressing a hand to his belly, his expression so young and carefree.

I was stunned. The lightness in his countenance changed it entirely, from one of granite to a waterfall.

Beautiful and captivating, he reminded me of a mirage, like in stories my father had told me of the desert. The sand plays tricks on your eyes, luring you in with promises of salvation, only to trick you and lead you to your demise.

"Yours is some of the best cooking I've ever tasted, so please, whatever you need to keep me fed, you let me know."

"Yes, sir. And do tell me if you have any preferences."

"I'll have a list for you, too, Evelyn," he said with a wink.

If I wasn't mistaken, Evelyn might have blushed. But I couldn't tell for sure, as the White Wolf turned his attention to me. The men had returned to clean the blood, and he snapped at them.

"Take the meat first before you smear it with blood," he said.

The growl in his voice raised the hairs on the back of my neck. Maybe it was the legends, but something in his tenor reminded me of a wolf.

More ayes, and both men were staring at the floor, utterly submissive.

He never broke my gaze as he crossed the kitchen in three long strides, while avoiding the blood, to stand inches from me. I could see why the nickname stuck, with his teeth on display as he snarled angrily at me, his handsome face creased with it.

His long hair was held back in its usual braid, the thick rope trailing from the top of his skull to midway down his back. Freckles adorned his nose and forehead in a way that made me think of the blood that splattered the floor. His broad cheeks and square jaw were locked in aggression, but it only lent to his attractiveness. Even his eyes, so cold and emotionless—the eyes of a killer.

If he thought I would cringe, he had the wrong woman.

As he placed one enormous hand around my throat, I put every ounce of fire I had into my eyes. Let him squeeze the life out of me; there was no more honorable death than defending those who couldn't protect themselves.

Admittedly, calling Evelyn defenseless was doing her an injustice.

"If you ever dare to order me around again," he said in my ear, his deep voice reverberating down my spine, "presume to tell me how to lead my men or any other *insolence*, I won't be so forgiving the next time, Sarah. Do you understand me?" he finished, squeezing off the air supply to my lungs to accentuate his point.

His face was inches from mine, and he smelled like snow and the wild, that scent that only existed in the depths of the forests. From what I could smell before my airway was constricted enough that no more airflow could be had, anyway.

A nod was all I could manage, and he loosened his grip, though he didn't let go yet. He searched my face for a moment, and my first pang of fear clanged through me. I didn't think I'd met the White Wolf before, but that didn't mean he hadn't seen me. If he recognized me, what would happen?

His anger flickered to something akin to amusement, and a smile erupted on his face. Suddenly, I couldn't recall my outrage—or my name.

Despite myself, my heart beat a little faster at the intimacy of his touch. Now that he wasn't threatening me, it *was* intimate, a caress. There was a possessiveness behind his hold.

Those blue eyes were as clear, cold, and fathomless as the winter sky. His nose was straight and slender, with no sign of a break despite his profession, and the freckles that radiated outward to his high tanned cheekbones looked more boyish this close.

His fair hair was braided back loosely today, adding to the boyishness I now witnessed. And his smile. Full lips framed a row of straight white teeth, his elongated canines enhancing his wolfish appearance.

I blinked and swallowed, partly because of my reaction to him and partly because of embarrassment. Then again, it was also due to his response to me.

He stood there, one hand on my throat, for much longer than necessary. He continued to scan my face, though for what, I wasn't sure—maybe he was waiting for me to look away, giving him my submission. We would be here forever if that was his goal.

It wasn't until the men could be heard coming from the cellar that he stepped away. The hand around my throat moved up to cup my cheek, and he patted it before sending me a little smile as if to dare me to disobey him.

Despite myself, I smiled back.

# CHAPTER
# TWO

My heart still thundered in my chest as Whalen made his way out of the kitchen, but not before shooting a warning glance at his men, who had reached the top of the stairs. Both had dinner plates where their eyes had been, their fear evident in the amount of white showing. Like two deer, they froze at his attention.

I only hoped that would stop them from bothering us more. I'd be a fool to think they wouldn't hold a grudge, but the White Wolf was as good a deterrent as I could hope for.

When I sent a glance of my own at the men, they had the good sense to look away, spines stiffening at my audacity. Good, let them think I was off my rocker; people didn't mess with the insane, as they were too unpredictable.

"Girl, I oughta take a chunk out of your hide for that," Evelyn whispered fervently.

"I'll not have anyone cross us, Evelyn," I spat as I turned back toward the sink.

"Not even Mr. Walsh?"

"Least of all that barbarian," I said, sliding my eyes toward the gentlewoman beside me.

The twinkle in her eyes was loud enough to call the cows home. I rolled mine in answer.

"I'll make that list," she said, waltzing away.

The wet sound of the men cleaning the floor sent shivers down my spine, and I turned back to the sink to rinse the blood off my hands. I wondered how much more I would have to spill before we would be done here.

I washed the dishes until my hands were red and wrinkled, sweat dripped down my chest, and the swirl of emotions was carried away too. As I scrubbed, I chastised myself for the whole of it.

The previous weeks weighed on me like a lodestone, bringing me down, down, down. Before the battle, we'd heard the news of the dragons and the supernatural horde, and that the White Wolf was steadily marching south. Why didn't we run?

We would have had a better chance at saving our homeland if we'd deserted it. Whalen wasn't bent on building an empire, so far as I could tell, but he would fight whoever got in his way.

Why did we stay and fight? If we had let him continue past us, my parents would still be with me, and Oisin would still be here.

Guilt thrummed through me like a dirge. Though I knew Oisin had been spared, I still hadn't a clue where he was.

I didn't have time for that feeling, though, and I tamped it down as quickly as it had risen. I had enough here to worry about. I couldn't help Oisin right now, as much as I wanted to.

The reminder left my mood black. All the emotions I thought had been washed away crept back on a phantom wind seeping into my bones. My earlier rashness added a layer of shame to the mix, squeezing my throat until my breath came in shallow bursts.

A man's life was forfeited because of me, and I wasn't sure how to feel about it. I busied myself at the sink with odds and ends while I sorted through the mess. It was one thing to take a life in battle, another entirely to cut a man down as I had minutes before.

The men had finally washed away the red staining the floor and were now wiping down the surrounding surfaces where splatter was still visible. Peeking at them under my arm as I rewashed a dish that didn't require it, I saw the anger boiling beneath the surface.

Their backs were straight, and they focused on their tasks, but the rhythmic scrubbing was short and brutal. They didn't glance at me or each other as they worked, and I hoped it meant they were mad at their fallen comrade more than me, his stupidity having finally cost him as they had long suspected it would.

That hope buoyed me, if only barely. I wasn't pleased to have had to end the man's life that way, but I wouldn't say I regretted it. Some people were past redemption, and he sure seemed that type.

I'd seen these men around the premises before. They were always to be found bickering or muttering to themselves if not outright causing a scene. Men like them were worse than murderers. They were cowards. They preyed on the innocent, stabbing anyone in the back who got in the way.

There was no use in mulling it over. It was done. Couldn't take it back.

My reverie was broken by Evelyn's reappearance, list in hand. I truly looked at her this time, and all that remained in the set of her jaw was resolve.

"I didn't survive this long without controversy, girl," she said, catching the concern in my eyes.

"Still, I should have been more worried about you. I'm sorry it took me so long to think of it."

"You needn't worry about me. That's why you didn't think to. You know that," she said, and the steel that glinted in her eyes reminded me of what lay beneath that gentle exterior.

"Evelyn, we might have been lucky so far, but I'll try not to push it."

"Love, every day we wake up is lucky. The rest is what makes life interesting."

"Interesting is one word for it."

"We've survived this far. What's a little longer? I don't want to be put in the dirt and have no one remember me. Let's make sure they know our names." She whispered the last conspiratorially, and I couldn't help but laugh.

"Now, you go take this list to Mr. Walsh, and be sure to leave an impression." She winked at me before returning to the kitchen.

The men's noise had ceased, and I waited for

them to depart before I dared leave Evelyn. When I glanced their way, only one looked at me, and the curiosity that lay in his gaze left me satisfied.

The look wasn't wary, nor was it malicious. I'd settle for being an enigma; people feared what they couldn't understand.

By the time they departed, so had Evelyn, who had disappeared into the dining room to tidy up, I assumed. And to be sure the rest of the soldiers knew we wouldn't balk in the face of danger, I knew.

Resigned to my task, I floated around the first floor. Men in various states of contentment or business were posted around the house.

Some lounged in chairs with a book, while others reveled at the dining table, laughing boisterously. Others were stationed at intervals, at the front door, the basement, and at each corner of the house outside. I hadn't wanted to ask where Whalen was, and luckily, none of the men seemed to note my presence and force me to.

The catch was that now I found myself creeping up the stairs to where I'd spent most of my life, dread snaking its way through my belly, with no idea if he was there. My parents' absence was keen, and the tears surprised me as I tiptoed up the stairs.

The bathroom was the first door on the right,

and my old bedroom was in front of me, but the latter's door was closed. Taking the opportunity, I snuck into the bathroom to compose myself.

It looked the same, albeit dirtier than usual, but the familiarity was both a balm and a burn. The comfort the space lent me dissipated in the wake of the despair that followed it, for it to be the same where nothing else would ever be again.

I pondered this as I stared at my reflection in the mirror above the sink. There had been other pivotal moments in my life, ones in which I looked at myself like I was doing now and knew deeply that the world I'd known was over and that this was a new one.

But none of those moments had hurt as much as this one.

Anger replaced despair, quick as a volcanic eruption, turning my blood to magma. I hadn't let anything hold me back yet, and I wasn't about to now. I'd honor my parents and my people's sacrifice or die trying.

The woman who stared back at me above the sink smiled wickedly before straightening her spine. I marveled at her beauty a moment before starting to walk away. She had never looked so wild and fierce, never so lovely.

Storming for the main bedroom, my parents' room, the one I'd been born in, I blew past my own room—the girl who had grown up there no longer existed.

I knocked once before opening the door, anger making me bold. Or maybe reckless was a better word for it. As the door opened, I was welcomed by swaths of bare skin and a scene I wished I could forget.

Not one but two women stood naked before the White Wolf, who was seated on the end of my parents' bed, shirtless but, thankfully, clothed from the waist down. The women hadn't a stitch on them, one blonde and one brunette, and were squealing their displeasure at the interruption.

Neither of them was the woman I'd seen braid his hair. I wondered how she'd feel about his extracurricular activities.

The White Wolf's eyes flashed yellow and cold in my direction, ire quick to make its presence known. If I weren't equally incensed, I might have backed down. I also might have wondered why his eyes looked yellow for an instant, as the blue now bored into me, making me wonder if I was imagining things.

Who was I kidding? No, I wouldn't, though a more intelligent person would have.

Pushing past the women who hurried to conceal themselves beneath the bedclothes, he crossed the room in three enormous strides. Stopping less than an inch in front of me, he peered down his nose at me, wrinkling it in a lupine way as he snarled at me.

"Are you so eager to join?" His sneer turned teasing, the truth of his words evident in his eyes. It was clear I was welcome to join at my discretion, but I wasn't to expect to be anything but a warm body for his pleasure.

I smacked the list in my hand against his enormous bare chest, the paper crushed in my rage. Not waiting for his dismissal, I removed my hand, and the paper fell to the floor between us.

"Your list," I said in my most saccharine voice, smiling like a madwoman.

His hand was on my throat again in an instant, shoving me back. As before, his hold was tight enough to threaten, not harm. I didn't even notice the wall as he pushed me against it, using enough strength to move me and enough restraint not to hurt me.

"Your mouth will cost you one day, darling," he said, his voice rough with anger and lust.

"Same move," I said, indicating his hand around my windpipe. "I hope you're not so predictable in bed."

He grinned, a savage thing. Gold shone from beneath blond brows; his hair was still braided, like the heathen he was.

"Come find out," he whispered, gaze darting to my lips and my body beneath them.

"I don't share," I whispered, looking at the open door.

"And who's calling who boring in bed?"

"Who said I don't enjoy being shared?" I asked, that sweet smile back on my face.

That did the trick. Anger flashed in those eyes so close to mine. His nostrils flared, his breath hitching with the adrenaline. A man not used to opposition.

He inhaled deeply and suddenly paused before leaning in to sniff me, my hair, my neck.

Gazing into my eyes, he searched them for a heartbeat, two heartbeats. On the third, he released me but didn't back up.

"Thank you for the list. Give Evelyn my thanks as well," he said, turning on his heel and heading back into the room.

As he paused to pick up the note before he shut the door on me, I had a great view of his chiseled back and behind. Narrow hips widened to fighter's shoulders, the massive muscles beneath shifting with every movement. Tattoos crisscrossed his tanned skin to the point where barely any open canvas remained. I idly wondered if tattoos covered his entire body; I'd been too furious before to notice his chest.

Now that I'd thought about it, though, I remembered tattoos and hair, blond and thick, peppering his chest and stomach and disappearing beneath the band of his trousers. His pecs were as pronounced and beautiful as his abs.

*Beautiful?* Damn it, why did I think his physique was stunning?

Who was I kidding? Because it was.

Even his face was chiseled and handsomely arranged. His strong jaw led to luscious, full lips magically seen through a full beard.

But the wildness that emanated from him left me still gasping for air long moments after the door had closed. Every muscle was honed from hard work and combat. The calluses I'd felt on his hands as he held my throat were deliciously rough against my sensitive skin.

And those eyes, again yellow as a wolf's, were undeniably vicious, but they called to me like a siren's song. I'd happily drown in them if I didn't despise the man.

Before pushing off the corridor wall, I told myself I was allowed to lust after a man, even if I hated him.

No noise came from the bedroom as I began to leave, so I was grateful for that, at least.

CHAPTER

# THREE

Morning came too soon, as I had spent the night restless. No position was comfortable enough, and every thought was worse than the last. I was angry, the kind of livid that made my teeth ache from clenching them unknowingly.

I wanted to hit things, flip things, and throw things at other things—the window, the door, Whalen's face. Oh, his handsome face had haunted my thoughts hour upon hour, and I imagined every scenario of what I wanted to do to him and what expression that face would have as I did it.

And every stupid thought of kissing that face only made me angrier. So when I opened the door to the kitchen at the crack of dawn to help Evelyn prepare breakfast and those haunting eyes were the first thing I saw, I nearly dove for the butcher knife sitting in the block on the table.

He didn't miss the look or the intent, and he angled himself between me and the table. I gritted my teeth, only to wince as my sore jaw protested the repeated movement.

It seemed he didn't miss that either, as he sent a concerned glance my way. After assessing me, he rifled through the drawers until he found the towels, then headed to the icebox, never turning his back to me. Smart man. He retrieved something from among the contents and wrapped it before handing it back to me.

I made no effort to accept the solace or the promise of peace that came with it. Holding my hand with his calloused one, he placed the cold towel in my palm and squeezed my fingers closed around it. I debated letting it fall to the ground, but something in his expression stopped me. He looked as if he was apologizing.

"Why are you up so early?" I asked, placing the coolness on my cheek, pointedly not thanking him for his kind gesture.

"I'm always up early." His voice was gruff with sleep.

"Haven't seen you," I replied.

"I'm seen only when I want to be," he said, smirking.

I believed him. The kettle whistled, then steadily climbed to keening. He grabbed it before it could raise the dead and poured the steaming water into a mug.

It clicked then. I'd woken to the kettle every morning, always imagining Evelyn in the kitchen. Had it actually been the White Wolf lurking outside my bedroom all this while?

He grabbed another mug, poured water over the coffee grounds in the sieve, and placed it on the counter closest to me. I stared daggers at him, and shockingly, he only laughed, a warm sound. And when he smiled, faint dimples could be seen through the swath of hair quickly taking over his face. Not a bad look.

"Sugar? Milk?"

I only nodded; yes, I wanted each of them.

He busied himself finding each item before grabbing a spoon for me and putting it next to the coffee before picking up his own. Taking a sip, he surveyed me over the rim of his mug, not jumping at the heat. I noticed that he drank his black.

After spooning in some sugar and milk, I went to place the milk back when he reached out for it. I warily left it with him before retreating to my mug to sip.

Damn it, if it wasn't delicious. He could brew a pot of coffee; I'd give him that.

He smiled in satisfaction at my reaction, and I scowled at him.

"Good?"

"It's coffee; even when it's bad, it's good," I retorted.

He laughed again, and the sound wrapped around me. So full of life, so rich and decadent. I inched a few steps away from him as if he were about to strike.

The movement stopped him short, and I almost got sad. Until I remembered that I wouldn't shed any tears for this monster.

"Right, then. I'll see you later, Sarah," he said, taking his mug to the kitchen door.

"Where are you going?" I asked before I could think better of it.

"Hunting," he replied softly, opening the door to the blustery wind outside. He closed it softly behind him, not sparing a glance in my direction.

I drank my coffee silently, then fed logs into the hearth until the fire roared with life. Evelyn managed the menu, but I busied myself with the kitchen's usual workings until she appeared.

There was enough coffee left for her cup as well as a second one for each of us. And right when I was wondering if he'd been making coffee for us each morning, Evelyn strode into the kitchen, looking chipper as ever.

"You're up early," she commented, grabbing her apron from behind the door and fastening it around her waist.

"Couldn't sleep," I replied, and the bite in my voice stopped her short.

"What's wrong?"

"Has he been making us coffee every morning?"

"If by 'he' you mean Mr. Walsh, he has."

"And you've known this whole time?"

She smiled softly, and the gesture made me both furious and melancholy. I was angry that she knew about and accepted the kind offer, and also a little disheartened, as if she'd slighted me by keeping it from me.

"We have had coffee together nearly every morning, sweetheart, though I can't say he ever lingered nor said much to me."

"But why?"

"Why has he made us coffee, or why haven't I mentioned it?"

"Both."

"Well, I suppose there's a gentleman somewhere inside him that the grapevine has forgotten to mention. And I haven't brought it up because you're looking at me like that."

"What do you mean?"

"Like I stabbed you in the back."

I floundered, her words hitting their mark.

"If life has taught you nothing else, remember that people aren't always what they seem. But that doesn't only have to mean that they're worse than you thought; occasionally, they're better than you imagined."

"But, Evelyn—" I began, but with a finger in the air, she cut off the whining I was about to launch into.

"You're grieving, with every right in the world to do so, and I'll not take that from you. Someone will pay for what's been done to your parents and our community. But perhaps there's more to the story than what it seems."

"More!" I shouted then. "What more could there be? The evidence is right in front of us!"

"Says the woman hiding in plain sight. They see

a servant, and for all the world, you are one to them because that's all they've ever known you to be. But to me, you are much, much more than that. Perhaps Mr. Walsh is not simply the murderer you think him."

I had no retort to that, nothing but a dumbfounded stare. She patted my hand then, smiling sweetly at me.

"Grief takes time, dear. Take all that you need."

I wasn't sure what to make of that, so I said nothing, only smiled back—though sneered was more like it.

As I sipped my coffee, she rattled off the breakfast plan, and I mindlessly set about the tasks she'd laid out for me.

What did time have to do with anything?

---

THE MORNING PASSED IN A BLUR, AND WHILE WE WERE cleaning up after breakfast and already preparing for lunch, a knock came at the door. I motioned for Evelyn to stay put and maybe tuck herself away, but she resisted my command to hide.

Rolling my eyes at her stubbornness, I went to the door. She only lifted her chin higher.

I opened the door a fraction and saw Padraig's face scowling at me. When his eyes met mine, there was a smile within them, though his face remained grave.

"Sarah?" Evelyn said from behind me.

"It's Padraig."

"Oh, Paddy!" she exclaimed, using her moniker for him, as I heard her shuffle closer.

I'd long since thought they had a secret relationship, or perhaps a not-so-secret one if I was suspicious of it. Nonetheless, they were a pair, and their chemistry was palpable.

"Evelyn." He inclined his head toward her, eyes shining. "Sarah," he said as he tilted his head toward me, letting us know he had caught on to my guise.

"I've missed you," Evelyn said without embarrassment.

"Aye, you too," he said, his gruffness genuine, as if the strain hurt him physically.

"How can we help you, Padraig?" I asked, the real questions burning inside me.

How was Oisin? Where was he? What had become of our clan?

"Need a poultice; think one of the horses is getting an infection," he said, staring at me pointedly.

My breath hitched, but I held my thundering heart together. *An infection, damn it.*

"That's a shame. Can I help you dress the wound?"

"Not sure that's necessary, milady." He whispered the last word.

I shot him a glare. "Oh, it's no trouble; a woman's touch sometimes does the trick. I'd hate to lame the horse."

"Aye, Paddy, she's right. A woman's touch might be needed," Evelyn hedged.

I glanced at her gratefully. Though I didn't know Oisin well, the fate of our clan depended on the two of us, whether we liked it or not. I owed it to my people to help him back on his feet.

"A poultice, then," Paddy said with the huff of a man exasperated with fussy women.

I busied myself, waving Evelyn off. The components were accessible: a potato, an onion, a lemon, and ginger. I grabbed some old linens and washed them before donning my coat to follow the old stable master, my nerves suddenly spiking.

I wasn't sure what was making me so anxious, though. The thought of seeing Oisin was undoubtedly part of it, but other thoughts circled as I pondered the severity of the situation. If the White

Wolf had forgiven my one traitorous act, a second was unlikely to yield the same results.

The trouble was that I didn't know if I minded or not. While I was keen on keeping my lifeblood inside my body with my head securely attached, the danger oddly excited me. It felt freeing to fight, even in a relatively peaceful manner.

But if I were caught, would it be a rebellious act? Would Whalen even recognize the would-be leader of our clan? Or would Oisin be nearly unrecognizable even to me? His injuries may have altered his looks in the weeks since the attack.

My nerves ratcheted to new heights as I finished my task and readied to exit the safety of the kitchen. It was an exercise in skill to maintain my composure as breathing became exceedingly difficult.

After saying a brief goodbye to Evelyn, I barely registered walking out into the cold air as I followed Paddy. My brain was detached from my body, as if I weren't controlling my movements and my legs moved of their own volition. My heart pounded in my ears, and I realized it wasn't Oisin who set my pulse soaring but Whalen.

The fear of discovery was there, but so was the fear of change. If Oisin got better, we would rise against our oppressor as I had vowed to do all this time. But suddenly, I was not so sure I wanted to.

I'd grown comfortable in my new role—too much so. When we took back control of our people, I would be expected to take the helm with Oisin at my side, as was promised.

Before, I had hardly minded, perhaps never considering that it would become a reality soon. But now, as I made my way to my betrothed, the future seemed as if it was upon me, and I was ill prepared to meet it.

Paddy walked in silence beside me, leaving me to my thoughts. He glanced my way now and again, though, as if assessing me.

I knew Paddy well enough, though most of our conversations had only ever been niceties. Truth be told, I wasn't sure how much more remained to know about the man beyond that. I was certain that Evelyn would be privy to another side of him, but that side was reserved for a spare few.

He was never cold to me, though, only reserved. And as he continued to lead the way, he seemed content enough in silence that I let him be.

The day was new, and the cold air bit my face and burned my throat most deliciously. After the morning I'd had, the early stroll was a perfect balm for my rattled nerves.

What did Evelyn know that I didn't? What had she alluded to? Was it something she had been explicitly told by Whalen or something she had observed?

When it came to Evelyn, who knew? Her heart was as large and bottomless as the ocean. I couldn't claim the same.

She could have meant anything. Like Whalen was worthy of forgiveness, or perhaps that the righteous thing to do was to forgive him. Either way, I didn't know how one could overlook the things he'd done, even if I had all the time in the world.

The barn was set way back on the property, skirting by the edge of the woods. To the left were the open fields for the horses to run and graze in, as well as the pens separating the different animals. We had cows and sheep and a few pigs. Most of them were in the barn now, probably hunkered down away from the cold air. A flash of white told me a stray sheep might be on the far end of the property, one of the hungrier ones.

As I followed Paddy into the barn, my nerves settled into an eerie calm. Suddenly, my second skin slipped into place, that extra gear always lurking beneath the surface, the part of me that could handle anything thrown my way. If I wasn't mistaken, I walked straighter, my shoulders back.

The smell wasn't evident at first, the barn stench overpowering on its own. But the farther we walked into the space to where Oisin was somehow hidden, the more the putrid odor of infection emanated. That I could smell the infection was not good news, and Paddy risking our intervention at long last was even worse. The damage was beyond his abilities.

He'd led me beyond the stalls nearly to the back doors when he stopped near the ladder for the hayloft. I was thinking the place far too obvious when he instead reached down to where hay was strewn all over the floor and swept until he found a latch, a tiny notch in the wood big enough for a finger.

As he pulled on it, the smell of earth hit me first, laced with the sickly-sweet smell beneath it. The hay above the latch didn't move, nor did the hay around it, concealing the entrance.

It was dark, but a faint light shone faintly below, hidden from view above the floorboards. I imagined the earth hid the light, as the stairs that led to the concealed room below were packed dirt that had wooden boards stamped into them to keep their shape and offer a foothold.

The stairs were wide enough but steep, indicating how deep this clandestine room was tucked beneath the barn. Paddy said nothing as he began the descent, offering a hand to help me with the treacherous trip.

I accepted, ego barking but content to allow Paddy the duty his honor requested of him. To him, I was still the lady of the house and the rightful future queen of our clan. Indeed, it even pained him to allow me in this hovel, but he certainly wouldn't deny me anything.

The door to this basement hung on a piece of rope, holding it aloft to allow for easy closing upon entrance. As I walked, I grabbed the bit of string that hung on the end and pulled it along with me, holding the wood before it smacked me in the head. Beneath the wood exterior, though, the inside looked like an animal hide to conceal light and sound from within.

No noise came from the depths. Hesitantly, I made the final step into the dim room. I wasn't prepared for the other men to be there, though. There were four men, Oisin included, though the three accompanying him looked the better of the group.

Oisin was nearly unrecognizable from the man I had known. His brown hair hung limp and dirty across his brow, and his already pale skin was sallow and drawn. Though he'd never been as hale as the White Wolf, he'd never been so sickly either.

Fever racked him, sweat gleaming on his face and neck, and the men beside him looked worried and tired. Rocks were placed on either side of his neck and along his torso, a pile of them in the corner. In lieu of snow that had yet to pile up, they used the stones to bring the fever down, keeping the unused ones in the cold earth to rotate them out.

No one spoke, though none of the men looked surprised to see me either. Paddy must have warned them that I was apt to join him, too stubborn for my own good. As I looked his way, he seemed to be saying precisely that as he looked right back.

Inhaling deeply, I squared my shoulders and moved closer to Oisin. The three men scrambled out of my way as best they could, two of them fair and one darker skinned. All three bore the hallmarks of a soldier guarding their leader.

The third paused in his scuttle, grabbing linens I had yet to notice tucked beside other supplies, which included a ewer for water, a pot, and a few vegetables. He nodded at me, the linens held aloft, and moved back toward Oisin.

I maneuvered around to the other side of Oisin, and though he slept, he was restless with fever. His lips moved in silent muttering, and his eyes raced behind closed eyelids.

They all remained silent, but the man who had gathered the linens met my eyes with his own over Oisin's prone body, assessing me.

What he detected there had him nodding approval, his dark eyes shining with an inner light. Stubble covered his face and neck, further darkening his complexion, but for all the dirt that caked his face and hair, he was a handsome man.

He looked away then, hands moving in delicate ministrations over the prince's stomach where brown and red linens were strapped to him. He took out a knife and cut the fabric slowly, easing it away from the reddened skin beneath.

Oisin shuddered then, groaning and wincing while still in his fever dreams. The bandages had all but fused to the wound, haphazardly sewn as it was, the scabbing surrounding it sticking to the cloth and opening small patches anew.

The injury was a hideous thing, crooked, gnarled, and angry. The skin was puckered and too tight, and the smell increased as the covering was pulled away. Reaching out a tentative hand, I felt the heat coming from it without ever touching his skin.

The soldier reached behind him to grab the ewer of water and handed it to me to pour over the wound. Inspecting the contents of the jug, I found it clean and clear, and I could feel his gaze on me as he waited expectantly for my approval. I met his gaze, and the pride he exuded over his meager accomplishment warmed my heart. He cared a lot for Oisin.

As I poured unhurriedly, he reached out to gently squeeze around the wound, allowing the buildup of infection to wash away with the water. Slow work, but luckily fresh, bright blood spilled before we were through.

Next, I gently and carefully applied the poultice amid Oisin's increasing groans. When it came time to bandage his torso again, the soldier took the reins, wrapping it with care and efficiency, a man used to the battlefield.

"Thank you," he whispered before I could.

His voice was deep but soft, as powerful as his ministrations, yet so gentle. Finally, he sat back, his work done, and I examined his handiwork with satisfaction.

"Thank you...," I trailed off, silently requesting his name.

"Joseph," he replied, then inclined his head to the man nearest me. "Michael." Then the next. "Donal."

"Michael?" I breathed, looking at Paddy, who nodded in confirmation.

I couldn't believe I hadn't recognized him, but then I also hadn't seen him in years. Last I saw he was a boy, wild and carefree with hair too long. But the man in front of me was a soldier, hair cut short and a beard growing scraggly in a coppery mess.

"Michael," I said as I threw myself at him in a hug probably improper for my status, but I'd rarely cared for those things before, much less now. He gripped me back equally tight, and tears sprang in my eyes.

A few years younger than me, I'd seen him grow into a mischievous boy who was the bane and light of his father's existence. Paddy's wife passed some years ago of a cough, which led to Michael's employment with the Beirne clan.

Paddy worked long hours, and though we'd offered to hire Michael as well, Paddy insisted he be a man on his own, and Oisin's family was more than happy to take him on. Which worked out, since our families were so entwined that it gave Michael something to keep his mind off his mother while still being close with his father.

These past few years, Michael grew quieter, losing himself in his work and refusing to attend the local functions. The last part was not surprising, though, as Paddy never attended them himself.

Somewhere along the way, Michael must have joined the warriors, and either the work or the sword training made him significantly more muscular. He was a grown man, and it was another thing to lament, the loss of the boy I had known. Though thank the gods I would get to know the man he now was.

We released each other, both a little embarrassed at the emotions we couldn't suppress. Smiling softly, I wiped the wetness from my eyes before taking a shaky breath.

In turn, I thanked each of them for watching over Oisin and defending our clan so bravely. And finally, for remaining here when the threat of capture could surely mean their demise.

We may need soldiers again soon. But first, Oisin would have to be healthy before we could think about those next steps.

It had been a quiet affair, and I spared a final

look at Oisin. Joseph stood watching over him, but he smiled gently at me as I followed Paddy out.

We didn't speak as he closed the hatch and tossed a fresh batch of hay over the area, nor as we walked out of the barn and checked surreptitiously for anyone lingering nearby until we were in the open field yards away. I wasn't sure I breathed until we'd gotten that far, and I had to take a moment to catch my breath before I spoke.

"It's going to take months," I said, careful not to speak too pointedly.

"Aye."

"You think he'll make it, don't you?"

"Not up to me, lass, but I sure hope so."

"Take supplies with you before you go," I said, still cautious despite the yards of open space surrounding us. I reached out to squeeze his hand, my silent happiness for him that Michael was well.

"Only a few," he said, looking sidelong at me. There was a softness in his eyes, his only response to my unspoken words.

I nodded, staring ahead again, lost in my thoughts.

If Oisin didn't make it, what would we do? I could hardly stay under Whalen's thumb, but what choice did I have?

I couldn't run and leave Evelyn behind, nor could she come with me if I did. But would anyone follow me to overthrow him? Or worse, was there anyone left to stand up to him?

I'd not considered that before, never seeing beyond Oisin saving us all. But he wasn't likely to save himself, much less the rest of us. And who remained beside the handful who I knew had survived? My resistance was moot if there were no townsfolk or anyone of our clan left.

I was unmoored, suddenly adrift in a gaping emptiness. Perhaps that was all Evelyn had meant when she'd said the White Wolf wasn't so awful. We could have been dealt a worse hand when no alternative existed. I had to deal with him or brave the unknown alone, without a familiar face accompanying me.

That was what those soldiers were facing as well. There would be no safe harbor for them here. They had only Oisin and the hope he represented or a fate similar to mine. Though at least they had one another.

We'd reached the house at last, and Paddy rested a hand on my shoulder before we headed inside, as if sensing the direction of my thoughts. His searching glance said enough, and I nodded in acknowledgment.

*I'm here. I'll take care of you both*, that look seemed to say.

I wrapped my arms around his neck before he could blink, and I smiled as his arms went around me tentatively but warmly. He was a man unaccustomed to displays of affection.

I let him go before he could shove me away, opened the door to the kitchen, and clambered inside to warm my chilled bones. Though not entirely freezing, the wind had torn through my clothes as if they were nothing, leaving me shivering as I hustled to the open flames of the stove.

Evelyn went to Paddy, and I watched their silent conversation as I held my hands before me. The situation was dire, but they would handle what came their way.

The conversation about the hidden room in the barn would have to wait. I'd known of the ones in the house but not elsewhere on the property. But I supposed my parents had assumed that if a disaster hit, wherever I was, someone would know the hidden room and sequester me away.

Sadness clanged through me, echoing in the hollow places they had left behind. I swallowed it quickly, my eyes burning at the effort. Little had my parents known that I would run toward it instead of away when disaster struck. However, they shouldn't have been surprised, as they had acted similarly.

"Paddy will need some supplies," I said, speaking on his behalf.

"Right, I thought that might be the case," Evelyn said, walking to the table where a basket already sat.

There was enough for another poultice and other items to stave off infection or eat, depending on what was necessary. Never mind enough food for a horse—fruits and vegetables filled it to the brim.

"Plenty in here. Deep basket," she said offhandedly. "Should get you by a week or so."

*In other words, more essential supplies are beneath if you need them—likely more clean wrappings, medicines, and maybe a few creature comforts.*

Paddy thanked her warmly, and I returned to the fire burning low in front of me. I didn't know what kind of displays of affection Paddy was apt to show, but I was not about to wait to find out. All I knew was that his eyes softened for Evelyn in a way I'd never seen from the man before.

I stayed there long after Paddy left. Evelyn's gentle footsteps shuffled around the kitchen, and I was lost in thought. I'd been so foolish, so hopeful that all would be well and I wouldn't have to suffer much longer. Only I hadn't considered that I had the good end of the deal.

Oisin had suffered dearly and still was, yet he was more fortunate than my parents and many of our clan who were struck down.

Eventually, I was nudged away and made to do some of the other chores before lunch preparation began. Sweeping and mopping were enough to last well into the lunch hours, and by the time I was finished, so was the food.

I'd worked up a healthy sweat and appetite, so as I sat at the table to dig in, I was disappointed at the bread and cheese. My body was craving protein after making do with what little we had for weeks. After exerting myself with the grueling tasks, my muscles were gnawing at me.

The door swung open while I was glaring at the empty plate after devouring my meager meal. Evelyn and I whipped our heads up at the intrusion to find the White Wolf staring back at us.

For that was what he resembled. His eyes were too bright, his face fierce and wild. The blood that coated his hands and clothes was fresh and red.

"Deer," he said by way of greeting, then turned on his heel.

Recognizing my cue, I got up to follow him. Broad shoulders met my gaze as I bundled myself with the cloak I kept at the back door. They were in line with my eyes, though I still stood just outside in the kitchen doorway, a reasonable five steps above the grass he stood on, the deer to the right of him.

The carcass had been expertly field dressed, the innards removed to help with the weight of carrying it back. It was a large buck, though, the thick legs and broad rack showcasing his burliness.

But the neck was also brutalized, the blood heavily coating the fur. If I wasn't mistaken, an animal had torn it out, severing the artery there. Glancing along the hide, I couldn't find another wound to indicate the bow Whalen had brought, though perhaps it was on the other side. But still, the neck wound was fresh.

"Never cleaned one before?" he growled, his voice gravelly.

"None without an arrow wound," I quipped.

His eyes flashed to mine, bright and angry. They looked lighter than I remembered, but they were gone in an instant.

He rolled the carcass over with a quick jerk of his arms, as if the thing didn't weigh close to two hundred pounds. A hole existed on the other side;

how deep, I couldn't tell, but he looked at me only long enough to ensure that I was satisfied before he turned the carcass back over.

"So you have before?" he queried again without looking at me.

"Yes," I said, staring daggers at his back.

"What are you waiting for, then?" he clipped, and I rolled my eyes before rolling up my sleeves.

Far be it from me to refuse to help when asked. I wouldn't be so petty—but that didn't mean I needed to be pleasant while doing it.

The work wasn't difficult, but it was much easier with an extra set of hands. Before long, we had the thing skinned and hung up in the shade of a tree on the edge of the property, close and high enough that predators shouldn't bother it, but far enough that no heat from the house would prevent it from cooling down and spoiling it.

Not one word was exchanged, not even in giving directions. We had moved as one, performing the complementary tasks without communicating, even when choosing the tree. I simply trailed him until he stopped.

The silence wasn't awkward either, nor was it strained. Instead, the exchange was strangely comfortable, as if we'd both remained silent only because we had nothing to say, and neither was compelled to do so out of politeness.

But instead of the lack of politeness being an act of aggression, it was more out of understanding. I contemplated this the entire way back to the house as we walked in that same bubble of quiet.

What did he understand from me in that silence? Or did he care so little about me that he didn't bother to consider me, and the reason he hadn't spoken was due to his complete lack of thought for me?

As if sensing the shift in my thoughts, he looked at me, his gaze evaluating. I threw him the blandest look back, and I could have sworn sadness filled his eyes as he continued to regard me. I broke the stare first, not saying a word.

"Thank you," he said, his deep voice soft.

"You're welcome," I replied, in keeping with my determination to behave appropriately, though I would have preferred to roll my eyes and walk faster to get away from him.

I went so far as to keep the mocking tone from my voice in favor of the monotone one I'd adopted. No emotion was better than any of the ones I was concealing.

A huff of air met my ears, and I peeked his way

to see his lips thinned. His eyes stayed fixed on the house, and it seemed as if he'd sighed audibly without realizing it. He could sigh all he wanted, but he wouldn't garner my sympathy with a few forlorn looks.

We reached the house before long, and he opened the door, allowing me in first. I said a quick thank-you, and he grunted in answer.

"Wash up outside," Evelyn said, hand on her hip, anticipating my grumbling. She wasn't wrong about my need to wash up or my irritation at doing it in the cold water and air, so I waved one of my bloody hands and turned around to storm back out the still-open door.

Only to slam into a wall of muscle standing behind me that I had stupidly forgotten about. Strong hands gripped my waist to keep me from falling backward as my own hands, formerly held up to wave off Evelyn, met the chest I had so carelessly run into.

When I recoiled like I had been burned, his hands tightened further, assuring my footing before letting go. I gritted my teeth, damning the flutter that radiated from my belly at his touch.

"We'll wash up in the creek," Whalen offered,

the timbre of his voice sending a new flurry of hormones through me.

It seemed as if he'd said it to save me from the whirlwind I found myself in.

He stepped out, holding the door for me to follow, and I numbly obeyed, putting one foot in front of the other as my heart tried to resume its normal beat. A feminine hum echoed from the kitchen, but I was too flushed to pay the noise any mind as the cool air embraced me again.

"Are you all right?" His voice caressed my right ear from where he walked beside me, a mountain of a man.

*And no less brutal,* I reminded myself tartly.

"Fine, thank you," I spat back, walking faster toward our destination.

He grasped my arm then, yanking me to him. I grabbed him, my fingers digging into the solid muscles of his forearm and bicep. He was so forceful, it was all I could do to stay upright.

"What is your problem?" I exclaimed, trying to step away from him.

That was when I noticed his face and the seriousness it held. Following his line of sight, it wasn't hard to understand what had caused his alarm.

A mother bear stood with her two cubs across

the small stream of water cutting through the lawn. It was early in the season for her to be out of hibernation, possibly due to a tumultuous month here. If she'd been sleeping nearby, there was a chance the bloodshed had wormed into her subconscious.

That smell was still on each of us.

A bear alone wasn't a terrible sight, but a mother with her cubs was a death sentence. And if she thought we were wounded, she'd be more inclined to attack.

That she was already standing wasn't a great sign. My heart beat in my throat, but I didn't move, not even to extract myself from his grip, though truthfully, the touch was comforting at the moment. If only I had thrown him in front of me as I ran in the other direction.

A low growl came from the bear. No, the noise was too close. I moved my hand closer to Whalen's chest so slowly, it was strangely intimate, my palm roving over every divot beneath his clothes to feel the vibration coming from him.

I didn't dare look, not as the bear got down onto all fours and bared her teeth in our direction. The rumble began again in earnest beneath my hand, the intimidating noise from him making fear trickle down my spine.

But amazingly, the sow ushered her cubs away from us while turning back to look the entire time. Only when she was beyond the rock wall that served as the border of our lands did either of us exhale a sigh of relief.

He loosened his grip but did not relinquish me, pulling me to face him fully. My hands slid off him, and I was self-aware enough to admit I missed the feeling of Whalen immediately. Oisin's arms weren't as thick and solid as his.

"You're not to be out on your own," he ordered, and I rolled my eyes. "I'm not asking," he said, that same growl lacing his words.

But the inhuman growl wasn't what caught my attention that time; the yellow flash in his eyes was what got me. I must have looked startled, too, because the color vanished as quickly as it had come, and his eyes softened with concern.

"Your eyes...." I stepped to the side, trying to see them at a different angle.

When he turned his head from me, I couldn't help but think his movement was very lupine. I reached out to guide his face back to mine, but he snatched my hand from the air before I could.

"It's true, then," I whispered.

He only bared his teeth, glaring at me. This close,

his eyes were more blue than they were yellow, but I couldn't mistake the change this time.

"How?"

"There's a lot you don't understand about this world, *Sarah*," he said, and I could have sworn he'd added an extra emphasis on my name.

"The dragons...."

"They're part of it."

"Part of what?"

"The stuff you don't understand," he said, and his eyes crackled like lightning as they met mine again, trying to will me to back down.

He had the wrong woman for that.

"Enlighten me," I said, giving my eyes the same fire that his held and taking a step closer to him.

The White Wolf didn't budge, but the anger turned into something wicked as he brought his face down to mine. I refused to balk even as our breaths mingled, though my own may have hitched slightly —a fact he didn't miss.

"It would be my pleasure," he whispered, his white teeth on display in a wolfish grin.

"Oh, you bet it would," I said with a wink and a sashay as I turned away from him to saunter toward the water.

One strong hand on my bicep kept me from my spectacular exit as he held me firmly. I twisted back to glare at him, but his face had none of the tension from the bear encounter nor the playfulness from seconds before. Instead, a weariness held them in its grip, making him look older than his years.

"You and Evelyn aren't to be out alone, okay?" he asked as those eyes, now blue again, begged me to obey.

"All right," I said, unwilling to give him more.

But as I turned to go, he tugged again—a gentle thing but no less forceful.

"I understand, Whalen," I said, giving him my guileless expression.

I'd expected amusement, but I found none. A sad smile graced his lips instead.

"Thank you," he whispered, letting me go, then walking toward the water himself.

I had anticipated that wicked smile at my innocent look and was shaken by its absence. What could have him so concerned?

I followed him to the creek and winced as the cold water kissed my skin, so soft and gentle yet so simultaneously jarring. Moving quickly, I scrubbed vigorously, cursing at the stubborn spots as I tried to clean myself thoroughly to avoid more of Evelyn's chastisement.

When I finished, I flung my hands around to dry them as well as I could before wiping them on my pants. However, no amount of drying could keep the coldness from seeping through the material, and I shivered violently as my frigid hands met my thighs.

He chuckled, and I rolled my eyes at him. Finished cleaning and drying his own hands, he came to me where I was still shivering and, to my surprise, threw his furs around my shoulders.

The warmth seeped into me immediately, his body heat still trapped in the animal hide, the thick pelt blocking all wind. My teeth stopped chattering within seconds.

"Thank you," I whispered, too cold to care that this was the man I hated. Maybe I should keep the furs. That might be a step toward revenge. Or perhaps I liked the luxurious feeling of the coat covering me down to my ankles.

"You called me by my name," he said, and his voice had a note of wonder.

"That's the point of them, isn't it?"

His soft chuckle met my ears, low and gentle, a welcome sound.

"People never use my name, too intimidated to dare, especially after they've witnessed my true nature. Yet here you are, using it sarcastically," he said, glancing at me sideways.

"I don't know what difference it makes, using your name," I said truthfully.

"I never did either, but some take offense at the familiarity it presumes."

"Should I not address you by your name, then?"

He seemed to consider it a moment. Or me—I couldn't tell by his expression.

"I enjoy my name on your lips," he said softly, his eyes wandering to the objects to which he referred.

I rolled my eyes, focusing on the path in front of us.

"Then I'll be sure to avoid saying it," I quipped.

He sighed then, and I couldn't help but look his way. I saw that sad smile on his face again.

"What is that look for?" I demanded, exasperated.

"More you don't understand," he said, quickening his pace to open the kitchen door for me, effectively ending our private conversation.

Evelyn inspected us both keenly before raising

her eyebrows at me. I looked back, bewildered, before she pointedly stared down at my torso still wrapped in Whalen's furs. I'd have thrown them off if he hadn't started speaking then.

"Evelyn, the meat should be ready in a couple of days. I'll head back out to get a rabbit for dinner tonight," he said, grabbing the hem of the hide I wore. "May I?" he asked politely.

I nodded. "Thank you," I said softly, dumbfounded. The anger I had clung to so viciously was mysteriously absent.

"You don't need to do all that. We have some beans that can get us through tonight."

"Nonsense, it's my pleasure," he said, standing behind me as he gently removed the cloak from my shoulders before throwing it back around his own. That same sad smile graced his full lips and shone in his eyes when he came around to meet mine. "Thank you for your help," he said, nodding at Evelyn before opening the door again.

"Thank you, Mr. Walsh," Evelyn said from the stove, where she stirred something in a pot. Her expression reflected his.

But he was already headed outside, ducking slightly to avoid the top of the doorframe. I wondered whether he would indeed hit it if he didn't.

I must have stared after him, because Evelyn cleared her throat, waking me from my reverie. Turning slowly, I found her sad smile replaced with a mischievous one.

"What?" I snapped, heading to the sink to scrub with cleaner water.

"You know what, even if you choose not to," she said tauntingly.

I rolled my eyes, finishing my second thorough scrub and drying before I turned to the vegetables waiting for dinner. My head swam far away from my body, and it took longer than it should have to know what I was doing.

He was a savage and a brute, a murderous thief. But even as I thought it now, I had trouble believing it. That truth made me angry in itself.

I chopped, sliced, and tossed the vegetables into a pot, and with every downward stroke of the blade, the anger bubbled higher. Eventually, I was throwing the damn vegetables when I was done brutally hacking at them, until tears were streaming down my face and I couldn't see what I was doing anymore.

Gentle hands came over my shoulders as Evelyn

turned me toward her in a warm embrace. Though not much taller than me, somehow I was cradled against her chest like I was no more than a child.

"I know you want someone to blame, but you might be pointing your finger in the wrong direction."

"Who, then?"

"I'd tell you if I knew, honey. Why don't you go lie down? Nothing to be done that I can't handle."

"Then it'll only be me and my thoughts," I said pitifully.

"That's important, too, sometimes," she said, gently squeezing me before ushering me along.

I obliged her. Worse than being alone with my thoughts was being seen as a sniveling mess by anyone else. Curling onto my excuse for a bed, I let the tears flow at will, hardly a coherent thought to be had as the levee broke.

At some point, I stopped crying, my thoughts still swirling around what had been and what now was—my parents gone, Oisin on his deathbed, and me a miserable mess.

I didn't know whether minutes or hours passed, but eventually, a soft knock came at the door. I'd fallen asleep, it seemed, and as I rubbed my eyes, I yawned, unsure of the hour.

I opened the door slowly, and my heart plummeted the second I saw who was on the other side. The White Wolf stood there, a bowl in hand and a sheepish grin on his face. My anxiety must have shown, because his face dropped slightly as he offered the bowl to me.

"Rabbit stew," he said, a man of few words.

"Thank you," I mumbled, reaching to accept his offer.

"Sorry, I didn't mean to wake you. I thought you might be hungry," he said, glancing behind me at the room.

I noticed the second his eyes alighted on my bundle of blankets on the floor and moved to block his view. He looked curiously at me, but thankfully, he let it go.

"No, it's fine, I am. And I shouldn't have slept anyway. I'll be up late tonight because of it."

"You needed rest," he said, leaning lightly against the doorjamb.

"I suppose so," I replied, tension filling the air.

"Well, I won't bother you anymore. I only wanted to be sure you're all right."

"Not a bother," I said, surprised at myself for meaning it. "Thank you again."

"Of course," he said, sending me a small smile, his full lips quirking slightly before retreating.

I almost asked him to sit with me, nearly followed him to the kitchen to sit beside him and ask him all the questions that burned inside me. Instead, I stood there and watched him leave, sadness echoing through me.

CHAPTER
# FOUR

I'd eaten the meal in the room I shared with Evelyn, grateful for something hot in my belly. But now I had to take the empty bowl to the kitchen and tend to some of my other needs, something I was reluctant to do.

Whalen hadn't mentioned my eyes, so I hoped they weren't as red rimmed and bloodshot as they felt, but something told me he'd only been polite by not gasping at my hideousness. I trudged to the kitchen anyway, eyes downcast as I tried to hear who was speaking.

The gentler voice was unmistakably Evelyn's, and the thunderous one was Whalen's. My stomach dropped immediately, and I was wholly dreading this inescapable interaction. I had to pass them to reach the bathroom off the kitchen.

"Don't say no to be polite, Evelyn," I heard him say as I got closer.

"I wouldn't dare," she said with a laugh. "That one's been mine from the start, and that's where I'd prefer to stay."

The conversation halted suddenly. No doubt the White Wolf was alerted to my presence. In all the time I'd spent reflecting, that was one thing I hadn't had time to analyze: how the legend was true.

I suppose, after the trauma of it all, I had become anesthetized to the absurdity of it. We lived in a magical world, but there were limitations. Or there once were. Dragons and shapeshifters were among the few species rare enough to be considered myths. But that was no longer the case.

Knowing I couldn't avoid the situation, I took the last few steps to enter the kitchen. For whatever reason, my heart rate tripled, and I all but ran for the washbasin.

"Thank you for the stew. Delicious as always, Evelyn," I mumbled as I placed the bowl and silverware in the basin before beelining for the bathroom.

The worst part about it was thinking of the

White Wolf's extraordinary hearing. The kitchen door closed behind me, which helped a little.

With my eyes burning at my embarrassment and feeling frenzied, I finally exited the bathroom to find Evelyn alone in the kitchen. She smirked at me, guessing at my discomfort and finding it absurd.

"Don't look at me that way," I said, rolling my eyes.

"Don't roll your eyes at me like that."

"What did he want?"

She gave me a mocking look.

"Besides bringing us a few rabbits for dinner tonight—which, if I recall correctly, he hand-delivered to you—as well as securing venison for the foreseeable future, he was asking after our comfort here."

"What does he care about our comfort?" I asked with a wave of my hand.

"More than you might think, *Sarah*," she said, emphasizing the nickname to insinuate that I was being dramatic.

Maybe so, but the anger still lingered.

"What time is it?" I asked.

"Bedtime for me, but I don't imagine it is for you after that nap you had."

"No, I don't imagine it is. Is it snowing?"

Light was pouring in through the window, too bright for this time of night. I moved closer to the door, and the wind whipped through the bottom, chilling me instantly. Peeking through the curtains, I saw thick flakes falling lazily to the frozen ground. Much was already dusting the grass and obscuring the view.

"Seems to me it might be here for a while," Evelyn said, standing at the sink to look out the window.

"You think the horse will be all right?" I asked, looking at her pointedly.

"Oh, sure. There's nothing to do about it if not either," she said, looking right back at me.

"I worry we won't be able to reach him if it snows a lot. He might need more supplies before we can take them there."

"He got a week's worth already and can survive a week without if necessary."

"But he's so weak."

"Then he'll be sleeping."

We were at an impasse, and I knew the logic of her argument, even if I didn't like it. I rolled my eyes again, signaling my agreeing to disagree.

Evelyn took it as a good enough sign and began to wash the dishes I had left in the sink. I wandered to the table to wait for her to be done, which was only a moment.

She meandered over to one of the drawers in the kitchen then and pulled out a deck of cards. When she held it up to me, I nodded once. "Sure, let's play a game."

"Any requests?" she asked as she settled across from me at the table and shuffled the deck.

"Dealer's choice," I replied.

I knew a handful of games, primarily compliments of Evelyn. While she shuffled, I put on the kettle for herbal tea. We played a few games of twenty-five until she had beaten me enough to be the sole victor while we sipped our tea. If my heart were in it, I wouldn't have let her beat me, but my mind was otherwise occupied.

After my defeat, she cleaned up our mugs, and I put the deck away. She gave me another sharp look before shuffling off to bed, my last warning to behave myself.

We both knew better than that.

The snow continued to float from the sky. Fat crystals of frozen water piled on their fallen comrades, obscuring the view of the land beneath it.

As I peeked out the window in the back door, the brightness shocked and delighted me. Moonlight reflected off the white landscape, giving the illusion of daylight. I loved very few things more than snow as it fell, especially as thickly as this.

Evelyn knew arguing with me was moot, so she hadn't. She'd only told me my idea was silly, pointless, and dangerous. But we both knew I would do what I wanted to do, regardless.

I didn't know whether my venture was from a place of concern for Oisin or out of boredom. Perhaps I'd wanted to be helpful, to enact change in a world that was out of my control. I had to obey that urge to tackle that which was within my control.

I heated the kettle again and put the hot liquid into a bladder before tucking it against my body to keep it warm in the bitter night air. After grabbing a few other essentials we could spare, I wrapped my coat around me as tightly as possible.

Slipping out into the night, I panicked as I made those first few steps outside. The wind blistered like a shard of ice against my skin. But the fear settled down the second I basked in the heavy snowfall, the flakes gently gracing my hair and skin, melting softly and smattering my face.

My long lashes held on to them like a daydream so perfect and fleeting that they didn't want to let go, but they melted anyway, beyond my reach. The woods were from a fairy tale, picturesque in the glow from the moon shining on the white snow in the trees and forest floor, forbidding and inviting.

I savored the moment for one more breath, and then I pushed on, ready to carry out my mission. The hot water bladder kept me particularly warm, but I worried that it cooled with every step I took, the heat leaching out of it as it tried to keep my internal temperature up.

I wrapped my hands around it through the cold, as if I could keep that precious heat in longer. Truthfully, it would only keep for an hour or two. It was a fruitless effort, but a comfort all the same.

Finally, the barn rose in my vision, and I quickened my pace. My heart began its staccato again, a steady thrum as the fear attempted to drench my senses. My brain refused to allow it until I was near safety.

I'd made this trip thousands of times, but my home no longer seemed safe like it had all those times before. Of course, there was always an element of nerves in being out at night, the dark shielding potential danger from sight, but the fear was heightened now.

I scurried into the barn and finally stopped

when the door closed behind me, panting with the adrenaline that scorched my veins. I was safe inside the barn. I had to calm my senses before heading down to deliver my wares.

Creeping softly once my breath evened out, I found the trapdoor, knocking gently to alert the men inside. Slowly, I lifted the latch as a light wavered from within, rising to bathe my face in its glow.

Joseph's gaze met mine, and he breathed in relief as he backed away to allow my entrance. As I hurried down, the stench alarmed me again. The space was dank and chilly, not conducive to proper healing.

Oisin was barely awake, his lids heavy with exhaustion, but he peered at me warmly. It seemed I'd woken everyone except Joseph, whose dark eyes were tired but alert.

"Emer," Oisin said, his voice a rough rasp.

"I'm glad you're awake."

"I'm told I have you to thank for that."

"I may have helped, but it's up to you."

"And you're back to help again?"

"Yes," I said, unloading my wares, including the hot water bladder tucked tightly against me. I felt its absence keenly.

Joseph reached over to take the items and moaned appreciatively at the heat.

"You are a benevolent queen," he said, his eyes dancing with amusement.

"I wish I had more, but I hoped this would help heat the whole space," I said with a frown.

"It's much appreciated," Michael said, his voice tinged with emotion.

I bit my lip, feeling uncertain.

"I'll let you rest. I only thought I would make you more comfortable. There's a nasty storm outside, so I don't know when anyone will be able to bring you more supplies."

"Then why did you risk yourself in such a storm? Snow, I'm assuming?"

"Yes. And because I'm hardly the one risking anything here."

"You can get lost, or worse, fall down and be buried by the snow," Oisin chided.

"Come, I'll walk you to the door," Joseph offered.

"No, please. I don't want to risk you being found on my behalf. I've lived here my whole life, and I can make it to the house. Thank you, though."

"I wouldn't mind seeing the outside world," he said with a wink, and I sighed, resigned.

With a final wave to Oisin and the men, I headed

back up the ladder. The brief visit was not as calming as I had hoped, but I was glad Oisin was awake without a fever.

Joseph followed quietly, shutting the hidden door behind himself. We walked silently to the barn door before peeking out. The flakes were falling in earnest, and the wind had settled, making a peaceful sight. But I knew the beauty could still hide dangers.

"I'm grateful to you for his health returning, but it's much too risky to come too often," Joseph said, a sigh escaping his lips.

"I know," I breathed. And I did, but I was too stubborn to take someone else's word on it.

"It makes me anxious that you're about to head out there alone."

"Don't be. I'll be fine," I whispered, unsheathing a knife at my hip.

"If anyone or *anything* gets that close to you, you're already in trouble," he admonished. "This may be your home, but it's different now. I can see the light from the house from here. Would you please flicker it once you're safe?"

"Of course, but stay hidden, please! I can't know if you're safe unless I come out here to check on you."

"Paddy will keep you updated. Now hurry along before it gets worse."

Indeed, the snow now fell in a constant flurry, making it difficult to see a few feet in front of me. If only the light were on at the house now to guide me.

"Wait, how do you know you can see the light from here?"

He gave a sheepish grin.

"I can't stay in that hole in the ground as well as the others can," he whispered apologetically.

"Neither could I," I answered honestly.

"Now go," he said with a flick of his hand.

I rose up to hug him before I left, which surprised us both. He caught my waist easily enough, though, and squeezed me gently before I scurried away into the cold.

The flakes were marvelous, and I was instantly coated in a layer of them. I imagined I was a fairy floating around in the woods, out in the elements and more alive for them.

But the pang of fear followed quickly. That was always the way. The journey to an exciting destination was filled with wonder, but the trip back could often be dreary at best and fearful at worst. This was one of those worst ones.

Quickening my pace, I put my head down

against the flurry. My breath sped up involuntarily until it came out in great puffs of air, too shallow to catch my breath as I choked on the adrenaline.

Glancing up to check my progress, I tripped, my arms flailing out to catch myself. The first thing I noticed when I recovered was bloodred streaks through the pristine snow, as if something had been dragged through it.

Or someone.

I scrambled to my feet and followed the trail slowly—only far enough to know that all was right, I told myself. Except no matter how far I went, the tracks went even farther until I could catch a glimpse of some figure moving beyond.

Common sense told me to hide, but to do that, I would have to get closer to whatever was there and then to the nearest tree to find cover. Instead, I stood stock-still, allowing my eyes to adjust while remaining as silent as possible.

Sounds hit me then, wet, sloppy, and crunching. That was when my heart plummeted. Panic sharpened my eyesight until scales revealed themselves, gleaming in the moonlight, a tail curled around a large muscle mass, and sharp teeth and talons dug into a carcass.

The rope dangling from the tree told me that it

was the deer we'd dressed earlier, eaten at last, I supposed. A chain dangled from the dragon's neck, slick with blood from its difficult escape.

I was glad to find only the deer and not a person. Not yet, at least.

I backed away slowly, hoping the dragon was distracted enough by its meal for me to slink away. I made it a few steps before something warm brushed against my legs, and I nearly screamed, but self-preservation kept me silent.

The knife at my side was in my hand in a flash, angled toward this second threat. Something wet and warm nuzzled against my ear, and I turned to figure out what was there.

White fur blended against the snow so perfectly, I could hardly tell where one ended and the other began as the flakes continued to fall on us. Yellow eyes met mine in a look of admonishment that swept away the horror, if only for a moment.

Eyes that were too intelligent and too familiar looked toward the house pointedly. Dumbfounded, I stayed rooted to the spot.

Larger than a wolf ought to be, he stood nearly to my shoulder in a strangely normal-looking way, as if by being smaller than this beast, ordinary wolves were somehow the odd ones.

He huffed, shoving me with his head in earnest. That's when I noticed the men with wolf banners on their surcoats surrounding the dragon, inching closer with chains and weapons drawn, hoping to recapture the creature of legend. I backed away a step, and the wolf inclined his head as if to say, *There you go, now—hurry up.*

But it was already too late.

I wasn't the only one to notice the men creeping forward. The dragon reared his head toward me since I was the closest danger to him, maw gaping. The dark recesses of his mouth began lightening, until flames could be seen pluming out of his mouth, directly at the wolf and me. Teeth sank into my forearm, firmly but not painfully. I was dragged backward a few feet, managing to stay upright only by the beast angling behind my back, his jaw on my left arm with his tail beyond my right one.

At the last second, though, the nearest soldier caught the beast's attention, and the flames erupted in a torrent of orange and yellow as they seared the man. His shout rent the air, causing the other men to panic as their comrade ran, trailing flames. I hadn't even noticed the man, and I was so startled, I was rooted to the spot.

The beast beside me pulled me relentlessly

again, but still I stood there in a daze, watching the scene unfold. As the man ran past near where I stood, fire surrounding him, I finally came out of my stupor and kicked one leg out at him, tripping him into the snow.

Flames sizzled, but some still licked at his exposed side, and I got onto my knees, released from the wolf in my effort, to dump snow onto him as fast as possible. Slowly, the flames fizzled out, but I could already see the exposed skin beneath—it was bubbled at best and missing at worst.

It seemed I wasn't the only one frozen, though, but as more flames erupted, we all seemed to shake it off. Men raised their shields and launched attacks on the dragon. None could get close enough, but the men wielded spears, backing it into a corner.

With that situation managed, I turned my attention to the man on the ground and saw he was coming to his senses. To his credit, he wasn't panicking the way I thought he might be. He had turned away from me and was assessing the damage to his right side.

"Let's clean you up," I said gently so I didn't startle him.

But when he turned to look at me, I was alarmed. Joseph looked back at me guiltily. Behind me, a low growl sounded, further shocking me, and I jumped at the noise.

Inserting himself between us, the wolf shoved me back and away, moving me relentlessly toward the house as he continued his warning to Joseph.

I pushed back, though, determined. "Quit it! He needs help."

Beside us, fire lit the night as the dragon fought his would-be captors. Already, one mighty wing was secured with thin chain mail and heavy weights attached at the bottom to prevent an aerial escape.

The wolf's answering growl was vicious, but I wouldn't relent, going around him to get to Joseph. It seemed I'd won the battle, as the wolf clamped massive jaws around Joseph's collar and pulled him back toward the house in a very "then move it already" way.

Joseph gritted his teeth but did not cry out, struggling to his feet painfully. A boom thundered, shaking the earth at our feet and knocking me down. In his frustration, the dragon flapped one mighty wing in an attempt to take off, then slammed back down with another earth-shattering crash.

Joseph stayed upright, but the White Wolf had had enough, it seemed, as he lowered his mighty head, forcing me onto his back as the night sky was illuminated once more. The dragon snarled viciously, trees igniting despite the dampness. My stomach churned as it slammed against his back, and I had little choice but to grab onto the fur in my effort not to fall off, riding sideways with my head upside down.

Grabbing his flank as high as I could, I hoisted myself up more so my stomach wouldn't spill all over the ground from the force of the running. But before I could fully situate myself, he stopped. This time, he sat down, unceremoniously dumping me into the snow at the back stairs.

A huff of hot air blew the hair from my face as his eyes met mine in disbelief, but they left before I could apologize. He growled at Joseph, then tore across the snow in a blur.

What was previously a beautiful, serene snowscape was now more like a hellscape as flames licked up several trees. The dragon's blood smeared the formerly pristine snow one way, and Joseph's blood dripped the other way, interspersed with footprints, paw prints, and marks from weapons.

Joseph was suddenly beside me to help me, but I held up my hand as I saw the flash of white among the flames. The wolf was behind the dragon now, quiet and undetected. He launched himself toward the dragon, teeth and claws bared.

I gasped, getting to my feet in horror, as if I could throw myself in between to stop him. But those strong jaws clenched around the dragon's throat and held tight as the creature reared and bucked, the wolf sinking his claws in to better his grip.

That was all the men needed as they flung another net over the exposed wing, and the creature was brought to his knees. Flames melted the snow again, but the wolf had taken the opportunity to root himself to the ground, and men approached behind him with another chain to attach to the dragon's neck.

That was when a hand landed on my shoulder, making me jump out of my skin. I expected Joseph, but Evelyn stood there, a look of admonishment on her face.

"I know," I whispered, turning back to the men.

They'd secured the scaly neck, and huge horses came with a giant sled to cart the beast away. I wasn't sure how they would wrangle the monster onto it, but I hadn't the time to watch as Evelyn's voice rang out.

"I need your help fixing him up."

Guilt washed over me. I'd been too absorbed in the goings-on and hadn't focused on my savior, for he had saved me from the fire that had ravaged his skin.

Heading back inside, Joseph was seated facing the kitchen so we could better help him. Candles lit the space, but there was hardly enough light to see by.

"Come near the window," I ordered, albeit politely. The light from the moon reflecting off the snow was brighter than any candle.

He obeyed, wincing a bit as he did so, and I moved to carry the chair for him. He waved me off, carried the chair himself, and took his seat again.

"Off with your shirt, lad," Evelyn said as she tested the water she had boiled, ever prepared for disaster.

I grabbed the salve we kept on hand for burns, cringing at the meager quantity. We would have to be strategic to be sure we covered him thoroughly. I made a mental note to make more tomorrow.

Throwing the medicine on the counter, I aided Joseph in removing the cloth from his skin. It came haltingly, a sticky wetness that had to hurt as much as the burn itself.

When his shirt was off, I was relieved to find

that the worst was concentrated on his left shoulder. While some of it was still severe, at least he had
enough meat to handle it on his shoulder and upper
chest.

I didn't know how he managed to get away as
unscathed as he did, but I was grateful he had.
Outside, more thunderous booms sounded, and
shouting followed in their wake. I only hoped no
one else was injured.

Guilt rang through me as a specific face flashed
across my mind. Shaking it off, I focused on
Joseph.

"Why did you run after me?" I asked softly as I
watched Evelyn gently clean the wounds.

"You know why," he said evenly.

"He might have your head for this."

"Hush now, he won't," Evelyn interjected,
leaving room for me to start to work with the burn
cream.

"I don't know why you keep defending him," I
spat, anger rising like the tide.

"It seems we'll find out soon enough, so save
your salve if I'm to lose my head anyway," Joseph
said wryly as he looked out the kitchen window.

It seemed Evelyn had tied the drapes to the side
to watch the events unfold, allowing us a view of

Whalen's hulking figure as he stalked toward us. I went to meet him, bristling myself.

I flung the door open at his arrival and yelped audibly as he scooped me up, then shut the door behind us. I hardly had time to protest before he deposited me in the snow a few feet from the house, far enough to give us a modicum of privacy.

"Don't you dare touch a hair on his head," I said, my words laced with venom.

He quirked his head to the side in a most lupine way before narrowing his eyes. Eyes that shone yellow, I noticed.

"And why not?" he asked, calmer than I had anticipated.

"He came only to protect me and has suffered enough already."

"Maybe I ought to put him out of his misery, then," he said, taking a step forward.

Jumping up, I slammed my hands against his chest, I probably looked half crazed as the anger bubbled over. Fisting his furs, I pulled him closer, surprised I wasn't foaming at the mouth.

"It will be the last thing you do," I swore, breath coming in short huffs, my body tingling with rage.

"And who will stop me? You, who needed how many men to come to your aid?" he questioned, sweeping one arm cockily toward the men still whisking the dragon away.

"I don't recall asking for any help; you are only inserting yourself because you're a brute."

"Brute, am I? It's a shame you have a thing for brutes, then, isn't it, love?"

I rolled my eyes, shoving him with all my might. He didn't move an inch.

"Well, this *brute*, darling, rescued you whether you like it or not. After, mind you, I explicitly told you not to go traipsing about. Is that the way of things with you? I ought to tell you to run naked around the yard next so you might join a nunnery instead," he growled, closing the gap to glare down at me.

Snow continued to fall on us in the moonlight. As he stood towering over me, his nostrils flared, temper still close to the surface.

"Fat chance of that. And I don't remember you saving me. I do believe the man inside who is suffering for it is the one who did the saving," I said, guilt rattling me at the statement.

"Aye, the man inside—a man I've yet to meet, come to think of it. Maybe it's him I ought to be questioning. Perhaps he'll be more forthcoming about his relationship with you," he said, making to move around me.

*Was that jealousy?*

I gripped one massive forearm in both hands, holding on tightly. He halted but refused to look my way.

"Joseph's one of our own, sworn to defend our clan. He's only doing his duty. Don't punish him even more for my mistakes," I pleaded, deflating a bit with the weight of my actions. "Punish me, if anything."

He looked at me then, again in that same quizzical manner. Sighing audibly, he worked his jaw a bit, his features softening slightly.

"Seems to me you've had enough punishment already, haven't you?"

I didn't reply—not even with a nod. The response was in my eyes as he nodded himself.

"Do I have to assign one of my men to guard you night and day, or will you listen this time?"

"I'll listen, but...." I shook my head.

"Out with it," he commanded, and a thrill went through me at the forcefulness of it.

"What does it matter to you what happens to me?"

"Who said you were who mattered? Might be my men I'm trying to protect, unlike yourself," he spat.

The jab hit its mark as my stomach twisted in agony. I was trying to care for the men I'd recently found to be mine, only I had failed, miserably. I looked out at the snow, trying to feel nothing quickly before reality sank in.

He lifted my chin then, blue eyes meeting mine with a burning look in them. Studying my face long enough to make my heart beat a little faster, he let go after a few beats.

"And where have your men been? I haven't seen them around."

"Couldn't say," I said truthfully.

"Perhaps your boyfriend knows," he said, pulling his arm out of my grasp to go after Joseph. His long strides were difficult to match, but I was afraid of what he would do if I didn't stop him.

"Don't hurt him!" I shouted, chasing after him, but he plowed ahead, giving me no heed.

After slamming the door open, he tempered himself at Evelyn's presence. They exchanged a look before he turned to her ward.

"Risky move to distract a dragon unarmed."

"Didn't occur to me. Only hoped to keep her from harm's way," Joseph said, inclining his head toward me.

"Brave man," Evelyn said as she smoothed ointment over his dark skin.

"You'd think I'd know such a man, but I haven't had the pleasure. What's your name?" Whalen crooned, his tone at odds with his black mood.

"Joseph," he replied, and not one of us failed to notice the lack of the word "sir" afterward.

"Joseph. Noble name for a noble man. Where have you been staying, Joseph, that you caught our damsel in distress here and thought to come to rescue her?"

Damn it, I couldn't think of any good excuse for him. Panic rose in me, and I squelched it as fast as I could, but the White Wolf still noticed as his head snapped my way.

"Patrol. I was making my rounds when I noticed her," he lied smoothly.

Whalen whipped his head back around, getting in Joseph's face and halting Evelyn's ministrations with his frame. Inhaling deeply, he smiled as he leaned back again.

"Patrol, then, is it? At whose request?"

"Mine," Joseph growled angrily as Evelyn went back to her work.

I stood still, heart thundering, afraid to utter a word and negate anything he said. Whalen looked at me again, and the sharpness to his features dulled slightly.

"Yours. Sure. Where have you been staying, then?"

"The woods."

"In the cold?"

"I'm a soldier," he replied gruffly, shoulders squaring.

"Yes, you are," Whalen said, walking over to stare down at me, nostrils flaring again as a grin split his handsome face. "Well, then, I have an idea. Since you're keen on watching over our damsel here," he went on, one massive hand reaching out to smooth my hair, then cup one cheek softly, making breathing a little more difficult for me, "I think we ought to do some rearranging. Sarah here will take the bedroom upstairs so I might keep an eye on her comings and goings, and you'll be set up with a cot down here, so you can stay warm and help me in watching this one."

When he concluded, he chucked one finger under my chin in triumph as he turned back to

Joseph. He was setting the trap, knowing one or both of us would lead him to the rest. My breathing evened out as his touch left me even as I regrettably yearned for it.

"Kind offer, but I'm fine in the woods."

"Oh, Joseph, I wouldn't call it an offer. I'll have my men set you up in the dining room with the rest of them. Evelyn, please rest. Do you need anything after all this fuss?"

"No, thank you, sir," she said, and I narrowed my eyes at the small smile she shone at him, then me.

"It's settled, then. You, with me," he said, grabbing my arm and half dragging me out of the kitchen.

Joseph made to get up, but Evelyn stayed him with a hand on his chest. She whispered something to him that had him narrowing his eyes at her, but I couldn't figure it out before I was pulled along past them.

"You can let go now, you know," I snapped at him, frustration mingling with embarrassment. And a little bit of the annoying simmer at his touch.

"Oh, sure, at your command, darling," he said.

Instead of letting go, he yanked once, pulling me to him as he turned toward me and threw me over one shoulder. I landed with a whoosh of air and a roll of my eyes.

"Wouldn't call that letting me go."

"Like you stayed inside as I asked?"

For once I didn't have an answer as I cringed. If only I had listened, Joseph wouldn't be hurt, and Oisin and the other men wouldn't be in danger of discovery. Though Whalen had treated him fairly, letting him stay inside and not assaulting him or worse. I still didn't trust him.

He walked straight up the stairs, one hand firmly on my thigh to hold me in place. I tried to ignore the heat seeping through to my skin, my hip snug in the crook of his neck.

My thoughts trailed to how perilously close my intimate parts were to his mouth when he barged into my bedroom. I was surprised when he laid me gently on the bed, my breath quickening traitorously. I'd expected to be tossed unceremoniously, and some of my righteousness disappeared with the gesture, replaced with something altogether different.

"Learned your lesson?" he admonished as he stood above me where I was lying on the bed.

I said nothing, lips thinning in response.

"I'll leave you to it, then," he said as he turned and began to walk away.

"Why?" I questioned before he could leave, sitting up as I did so.

"It suits you, don't you think?" He gestured to the room.

He didn't wait for my answer, knowing full well that wasn't what I had been asking. As he closed the door gently behind him, I felt oddly bereft.

I'd anticipated a tongue-lashing—hell, maybe a real lashing—but I got nothing. The wind went out of my sails, and I was confused and agitated.

I was still in my coat, and I ripped the thing off as if it was on fire and threw it to the ground. What I wouldn't do for the relief he offered with his broad shoulders and sinful mouth.

No, that wasn't what I wanted, I reminded myself. I'd rather ram my fist into his gorgeous face, kick and scream and brawl until I melted into nothingness. My skin crawled with the tidal wave cresting within me, and still I sat motionless, staring at the coat on the floor.

Unable to take it any longer, I started pacing. My childhood bedroom looked remarkably the same as ever, and it strangely made me more unsettled.

I was sad, angry, embarrassed, and so, so lonely.

The loneliness was what crushed my spirit. I'd been lusting after the White Wolf for goodness' sake, simply to feel something other than empty and cold.

The tears came then, injustice drowning me in their wake. Instead of smashing furniture like I'd been daydreaming about moments before, I curled up on the bed, distantly noting the clean sheets.

THE HOUSE WAS ON FIRE. NOT A KITCHEN FIRE GONE AWRY but a blazing inferno, roaring and growling like the dragon who wrought it. I screamed and kicked, but no noise came out as I fought to get inside, to save my parents, my life as it had been.

My parents. My heart sank and renewed my fervor. I had to help them. I couldn't fathom any other choice.

Strong hands gripped my arms, holding me still, and I kept kicking and screaming. The only difference was that now when I screamed, sound came out.

"Sarah!" A gruff voice broke through the haze, and I opened my eyes.

I was in my room, which apparently was not on

fire, about which I was at first relieved. But that meant that my parents, whom I had been fighting to save, were gone already. My face was wet, but the bed was still made. I had fallen asleep on top of the covers.

"Only a nightmare, darling," he whispered, still holding on to me.

"Which one?" I asked sarcastically, meeting his gaze at last.

The saddest smile tugged on his lips before he let me go. Insanely, I almost grabbed his hand to pull him closer to me, to push the misery away.

"You've had a fright, that's all. It's still early enough that you should get some more sleep."

Light peeked through the windows. It was nearly dawn. Whalen stood there, boots and furs on already.

"I need to help Evelyn," I said, sitting up.

"You don't. My sister will manage this morning, as you've each had little sleep between the two of you."

"Your sister?"

"Aye—blonde, fierce looking."

I scrunched my eyebrows in confusion, not placing a face to his description.

"Bears a resemblance to me? She's the one who

keeps taming my hair, which keeps it from my face, so I allow it."

"Your sister?" I queried, the incredulity shining through.

He did smile then, a wicked thing.

"My sister, aye. And who did you think she was?"

"I thought she was your unfortunate paramour —one of a few, by my count."

"Counting, are you? And, darling, no woman considers herself unfortunate to share a bed with me, I can assure you of that," he said, slinking closer with no small amount of swagger.

Damn my breath. It had a mind of its own as I fought to keep it steady. His nostrils flared slightly, making me suddenly aware of why.

"I have better things to do with my time, thank you," I said curtly.

"Oh, perhaps spend it with your boyfriend, I take it?"

"Joseph is not my boyfriend. Nor is any man, for that matter," I said, biting my lip immediately.

Why did I say that? I was betrothed to Oisin, which I couldn't now retract and say instead because Oisin was a ghost to Whalen. If I'd have left it at the first half, I'd be fine, though it was none of his business anyway.

"Pity," he said, holding my gaze for a beat. "Well, I'm off, then. Go to sleep. You look half as good as you feel right now."

"Not up to your standards, I take it?" I asked, though truthfully my head was a lead weight, my body sore all over from the adrenaline.

"Darling, you meet every man's standard," he said, his voice deepening and eyes darkening.

My mouth went a little dry. I didn't even have a quip to volley back, my brain too sleep fogged. Or maybe it was something more, given how my blood thrummed uncomfortably, a steady beat building low in my belly.

"Go to bed," he commanded, turning to the door.

"Wait, where are you going? You didn't sleep either," I said, regretting it immediately.

"Want me to stay, then?" He smiled back at me, sizing me up.

"That wasn't what I meant," I said, cursing my fair skin because I was certain I could feel the beginnings of a blush.

I wasn't virginal—I'd had a man share my bed before—but I wasn't sure I was up to his level. My parents never placed importance on that aspect of my life, and I'd been free to date as I grew. Only none had held my interest, and my betrothal to Oisin had been a compromise with my parents in my lack of a choice among my suitors.

Yet, even if I were, these weren't thoughts I was supposed to be harboring right now or ever.

"I'm off to hunt; we need to replace the deer we lost."

"Oh," I breathed, somehow relieved for reasons I didn't want to delve into when a thought crossed my mind. "Do you hunt as the wolf?"

"Yes. Does it bother you?"

"Why would it?"

"Most people believe I'm the White Wolf only in nickname; they don't believe I can change forms."

"And most don't believe in dragons, and yet I've seen both."

"That you have," he said, pausing a beat. "Neither seems to faze you."

"Shall I hide under the bed? Would that suit you better?"

"No, you suit me fine," he said, reiterating his earlier sentiment.

I had no quip, so I said nothing. My body warred with my brain; it hummed its approval at his obvious appreciation, but I still wanted to hate him.

"What are you going to do with the dragon?" I asked to change the subject.

"We have a few chained outside a few miles away. We've been working on training them."

"Training them?"

"They can be, or so the legends go."

The legend was that a powerful witch would raise the dead again, villains of old to overthrow our ruler, Dagda. To open the portals between worlds and let magic and chaos reign. That dragons existed lent a certain truth to the story, sending shivers down my spine.

Other worlds didn't exist, not that I knew of. We had our beliefs of heaven and hell, but they weren't places you could visit and touch.

But as history goes, no evil would rise without a hero to meet them. Only, was Whalen the villain or the hero?

"What for?" I asked.

"What wouldn't a dragon be good for?"

"That's not the whole of it."

"No, it's not. But that's a discussion for another day."

"So you keep saying."

"You'll know when it's the day, and not any sooner."

I rolled my eyes, yawning despite myself.

"Sleep. Time enough later to talk," he said, and his eyes held a promise, making butterflies erupt in my belly.

"Good luck," I called as he made for the door, unsure of what else to say.

"Luck has nothing to do with it," he said with a roguish wink as he gently closed the door.

Sleep, my ass. How could I sleep with so much to consider? So many questions and so few answers.

He was maddening in more than one sense.

Training dragons? A wolf shifter training dragons.

I sat up then, my brain landing on a particular story my father had told. He'd harped on one above the rest that told of a war between worlds. That ours once was and would be caught once again in a fight with Bitu, the land of the living, and Dubnos, the Underworld.

Albios, where we dwelled, had been long cut off from the two. Dagda, the All-Father, had deemed it necessary after the technology he'd shared with the human world became advanced enough and it put us in jeopardy. Only hints of magic, simple spells, and potions had grown rapidly in their hands.

The schism had robbed us of much of the magic that existed when we drew from all the worlds, but the act was a necessary evil to prevent further atrocities from interfering with our existence.

But the story my father told was one of a war, a quiet kind. It snuck up unexpectedly, and the magic would well up softly and gently over time only to erupt like a volcano. Like the steady growth of a lake until it burst beyond the dam in a rush. Of ancient foes rising from the depths to let chaos reign once more. Most significantly, of a dragon who would sweep the lands, as it had centuries ago, bringing destruction in its wake.

But the dragons the White Wolf kept, though massive, were not the magnitude my father spoke of. Why would Whalen be training dragons? Where did he get them?

Thoughts swirled, but I yawned again, relishing the luxury of my own bed. How I had missed it.

It still smelled the same, too, as if the room encapsulated it.

I AWOKE TO THE FRAGRANCE OF COFFEE AND MY MOTHER, crisp air, and the warm smell of the vanilla she was fond of—just to remember that it was only the room that held the memory of her, my bedding and clothing she had tended for so long that her scent permeated through time.

Slowly I opened my eyes, expecting Evelyn to be there, warm mug in hand. My blood heated upon finding Whalen standing above me, smelling of the woods, coffee proffered in one hand.

His salacious grin told me he didn't miss my instant reaction to his presence, but fortunately he said nothing, only holding the cup out farther. I sat up, smoothing my rumpled hair in embarrassment and rubbing my eyes before taking his offering.

Our hands met briefly during the exchange, and lightning snaked its way through my body. I nearly shivered from the shock of it but bit my lip instead. He noticed that too. His eyes, intent on my mouth, darkened eagerly.

A heady thing.

I drank the aromatic brew, not only to break the tension but also to wake myself up if he did decide to join me in bed. It would be sacrilege if I were hardly awake enough to enjoy it.

Damn it, I wasn't supposed to think that.

"Thank you," I mumbled after a moment, feeling the liquid seep into my bloodstream.

"Of course," he said, then hesitated a moment, as if he was about to say something but thought better of it before turning toward the door.

"Did you get anything?" I asked, reaching for something to say. I wasn't entirely sure why.

"Huh?"

"Hunting. Was it successful?"

"Oh, aye, deer and a couple of rabbits. I have some of the men cleaning them today."

"Well, thank you."

"It's my duty," he said, going to turn back to the door. My expression halted him, though. "I was never after hurting anyone, Sarah."

My heart sank.

"You did, though."

"Did I? Or did I only hurt the people who attacked your clan?"

I didn't say anything, mulling it over. Strange to consider, and stranger still that I hadn't done so yet.

His expression turned to stone, but he said nothing as he gently closed the door behind him.

As I sipped the coffee, dread welled up inside me. All the anger and hatred, the sadness and loss came back with a vengeance that threatened to consume me. If what he said were true, and he'd only meant to protect me and my clan, then I'd been horrible to someone who had honestly been nothing but nice to me.

The memory of him with those women flashed through my brain, and I let the burn of it turn me bitter again. Though, if I were being truthful, his preferences in bed were hardly something I could judge him for.

Unclenching my jaw, I took another sip, trying to wait out the waves of misery as they turned the coffee in my stomach into acid. No tears fell—only the burning remained until it eroded all my emotions but one. All that was left was the hope-lessness draining whatever energy the caffeine had managed to muster.

I didn't know how long I sat there, but long after the coffee was gone and my stomach had begun growling in protest, Evelyn came to fetch me. She walked through the door after a gentle knock I didn't answer, peering inquisitively around the corner.

"You're not still sleeping, are you, lass?" she said, not accusingly but concerned.

"No, I'm up," I said, still lounging back with my

empty mug in my hands. I stared at it as if it held the answers to my problems.

"You'll not find anything by wallowing in your own misery."

"I'm not looking for anything," I said miserably, moving to get up.

Evelyn came over to hug me as I stood, and the hold I had on my emotions burst. Tears welled up, filled with embarrassment from last night and the loss and loneliness that still permeated my every moment both awake and asleep.

She held me as they spilled out, murmuring soothing sounds and phrases as she did so. I couldn't even say what had me so upset, but I knew deep down, I wanted Whalen to be the enemy I had thought him to be. But I was finding it more and more difficult to keep blaming him for everything that had happened. So who *would* I blame?

Eventually, the tears dried up, and she let me go. My eyes were puffy and red, and I needed to clean myself up.

"Thank you," I whispered, giving her a squeeze.

"Anytime, sweetheart. Now, when you're ready, come on down and eat something. The rabbit stew is divine."

"Is she still there?"

"Sloane? Aye, but don't worry—she's nice."

I made a face, not believing her, or rather not wanting to believe her.

She chuckled, and I felt like I was a kid again, being thought adorable for my dourness. I offered her a smile before she left, closing the door gently.

Rummaging around, I was surprised to find all my clothing and other things were intact. I grabbed a change of clothes and headed to the bathroom to clean up some more before I headed down. A real bath would have to wait, but for now, I did the best I could.

As I headed downstairs, it was oddly quiet, which was stranger still. I had gotten so used to the noise when previously my house was always peaceful. Walking past the living room and dining room, I saw no soldiers nor any evidence of any.

The cot Joseph had slept on was gone, as were the others. Only shadows through the windows told me men were posted outside in the cold.

Making my way to the kitchen, I heard voices floating out of the doorway, and I braced myself. I wasn't too keen on meeting someone with my face swollen from crying and still only half awake, especially Whalen's sister, whom I had thought was his lover.

Wincing, I took a deep breath, unsure if I hoped Joseph was there or not. It would be nice to have another familiar face, but I wasn't certain that I could avoid giving us both away. I hardly knew the man other than the fact that Oisin trusted him. If he even did, I didn't know him well enough to feel the same.

The trouble was, if he *was* there, I could hardly ask Evelyn about him.

Straining my ears as I got closer, I heard no male voices. Disappointment flooded through me, replaced by irritation a moment later. It wasn't Joseph's voice I was hoping to hear, I realized. I was such a mess.

Shaking it off, I straightened my shoulders and walked into the kitchen. Surely they had heard my approach already, so if I delayed any longer, they'd know I was trying to eavesdrop.

Evelyn and Sloane sat at the table, mugs of tea in their hands. Their conversation quieted as I entered the room.

"Sarah," Sloane said as she stood up to come shake my hand. "Lovely to meet you."

"Sloane, you as well. Thank you for cooking this morning—and afternoon, I suppose."

"My pleasure. Let me grab you a bowl—if you're hungry, that is?"

"I would love one, thank you, but I can help myself. You don't need to."

"Nonsense, go relax. You've earned it," she said with a small smile that made me wonder what exactly she had meant.

I made my way to the table to sit beside Evelyn, who squeezed my hand in reassurance. I squeezed back but turned my attention back to Sloane.

Her hair was a similar shade of blonde to Whalen's, but where his was braided and wild, hers was sleek and pulled back loosely to keep it out of her face. She was dressed in the same style as Whalen, with leathers and furs the mountain clans usually wore, but she held herself more rigidly than he did.

She turned her face to us after she filled the bowl with stew, still looking down as she grabbed a hunk of bread and the butter to go with it. The fierceness was there in the lines of her face, but kindness shone in her eyes too.

She bore the same freeness that Whalen did, and I was surprised that I didn't think them siblings before. The blue of her eyes held the same crispness as his, and the similarities continued in the bow of her lips and the shape of her brow.

And though she was infinitely more feminine than him, she still held herself with the same strength he did. Her shoulders were broad, and she was obviously strong, but she moved with ethereal grace and poise. I wondered if they had more in common than their looks, but no hint of yellow was evident in her eyes.

She came to the table and placed everything in front of me. I had to look away lest she read my thoughts.

"Something to drink?"

"Water would be fine, thank you."

She went to get me a glass and filled it with water, and I went back to studying her while she did so. Then she spoke.

"Yes, I share more than looks with my brother," she said affably.

I would have ducked my head if I weren't so curious.

"You can also change forms?"

"Aye, I can," she said, bringing me the water.

I mumbled another "Thank you" as she took the seat opposite me.

"Is your wolf white too?" I asked, my curiosity getting the best of me.

"Red, actually," she answered.

"Sorry, I didn't mean to pry."

"No, it's fine. I understand the novelty."

We were silent then while I ate some of the stew. It was delicious.

"This is fantastic," I said truthfully. I would be shoveling it in if it weren't still so hot.

Normally stew wouldn't be how I chose to break my fast, but it was much later in the day than I usually rose, and I was hungrier than I'd realized. I was glad they had kept it hot, too, seeing as everyone else ate hours ago.

"Thank you. My mother's recipe."

"She taught you well," I said, turning my attention to Evelyn to steer the conversation elsewhere, more toward what was occupying my thoughts—or who. "Where is everyone?" I asked, an innocent enough question.

"Whalen had the men relocated to another manse," Sloane answered for her.

"Oh," I said, for lack of anything better to say. I was afraid to be too interested lest she realize whom I was actually asking after.

"Yes. After what happened last night, he thought

it would be best to have his men guard the dragons more closely," Evelyn explained.

"I understand," I said, cursing at the sinking feeling that echoed inside. I didn't dare ask if it meant that Whalen was to stay elsewhere also. I wasn't sure I even wanted to know.

"It's nice. Not that the company wasn't welcome, only I'm more accustomed to a quieter home," Evelyn added.

"Me too," I echoed.

Sloane said nothing, only smiled gently.

"We're happy to have you stay, Sloane, if you'd have us," Evelyn offered, and my traitorous heart sped up.

If Sloane stayed, then perhaps Whalen would, too, instead of going to the other house he had sent his men to. My mouth dried up at the prospect of only one wall separating him from me at night. But my heart sank at her words.

"Thank you, but it's all right. I prefer to stay with my men."

"Your men?" I questioned.

"Aye, I command the men here, under my brother," she said, and I thought there was a hint of melancholy in her words.

Images flashed through my mind, ones I wished

I could forget, but I knew they were there to stay. My mother, my dream last night, the bodies of the men I had slain, the blood on the kitchen floor.

"I'm sorry," she whispered. "Mine were not the ones who hurt you so."

"What do you mean?"

*It wasn't her troop, maybe?*

"We were on the heels of another army, racing to prevent further bloodshed. It didn't work," she said apologetically.

"I don't understand."

"There's a lot I still don't understand myself, but it may not be my tale to tell."

"It's okay," I replied, looking into my stew.

I respected her not answering, but if not her, then who? What did she mean by two armies? Because I knew what I saw: giants with maces and dragons shooting flames at men and women alike. If they weren't her men, were they still Whalen's? Was that why she didn't want to elaborate?

Evelyn placed a hand on my arm, but I couldn't look up at the moment. She carried on, giving me the time I needed.

"Women don't normally command armies in our clan," I said to break the tension.

I would have asked her more about what she

meant, but I would save that for Whalen. He had a few things he had to answer to as it was, so I could simply add this to the list.

"In the mountains, women can hold any position," she said, taking the offering I gave to her. "Being a shapeshifter presented a unique opportunity. I'm not as big as Whalen, and frankly not as well suited to leadership nor inclined to lead. But the men look to me regardless of my own aspirations."

"Did you have other ambitions in mind?"

"Ah, well, the normal life calls to me, but I can't deny the power running in my blood."

"Perhaps you could have both?" Evelyn suggested.

"I can hardly run into battle with a babe in my belly," she said ruefully.

"No, I wouldn't think so, but it doesn't mean you can't have that as well."

"And what, wed one of my men? Even if one had caught my eye, it would hardly be appropriate."

"No, but when the right one strolls along, you'll know," Evelyn said with a twinkle in her eye that told me she was thinking of Paddy. "You don't decide when it happens or who it happens to be, though," she added, and I knew the last was directed at me.

Sloane looked at me, and I pretended not to notice the turn of her head, refusing to look up. Instead, I focused on my meal, spooning another bite into my mouth. It couldn't be Whalen. Lust, sure, but not love.

"I suppose you're right, but only time will tell," Sloane said, emptying the remains of her tea in one gulp before standing up to wash the mug at the sink. "On that note, I must be heading back instead of indulging myself in girl talk, though it was much appreciated. Some of the men will remain posted outside for your safety, but we'll try to stay out of your space."

I hesitated, but I knew it had to come from me.

"You're not a bother, nor are your men. Please come and visit as often as you want. And tell your men to stay inside if they're on duty, as it's much too cold to remain outside."

"Very kind of you, but it's not necessary."

"It is. I insist, and please come and cook for us when you've got a chance, because I've grown quite tired of Evelyn's cooking," I said, shooting Evelyn a wink.

"Have we been eating different meals? I can't imagine anyone growing tired of Evelyn's cooking," Sloane said amiably.

"It's like growing tired of sunshine, I know."

Sloane laughed at that but inclined her head.

"I'll tell them to come inside, but I won't order them to, and I'll break some bread with you. Not tonight, though—maybe tomorrow. I'll make something with the venison when it's ready."

"I look forward to it," I said, meaning it.

For all I wanted to hate her brother, I couldn't find it in me to hate this woman. *Not when she reminds me so much of myself*, I thought with shock.

"I'll see you out," Evelyn said as she stood up to follow Sloane, leaving me alone in the kitchen.

That hadn't been horrible. I wasn't sure how much I liked it. I'd secretly wanted her to be insufferable so I could continue in my rage and misery, but I was constantly being forced to be less cynical, and I hated it.

Evelyn returned after a few minutes, just as I was getting up to wash the dishes. Staring out the window, I marveled at the destruction from the night before. It looked worse in broad daylight, and I cringed at how close I had come to getting torched myself. Which made me think of Joseph.

"How is Joseph?" I asked as I washed the dishes.

"Fine. He was cleaning the deer. Whalen told him he wasn't obligated to, but the lad insisted on being useful."

"How do the burns look?"

"Less severe. We'll need to make more salve today."

"Good. Do we have everything?"

"No, but Whalen is getting a honeycomb," she said, looking at me as she did, as if to say, *See? He can't be all bad.*

I nodded. I could tell it wasn't the reaction she was hoping for, but it was an improvement, nonetheless.

"I'm going to go see how Joseph fares," I said. There was little else to do, since most of the duties had already been carried out.

"Whalen wants you to stay put. I wouldn't mind it myself. Perhaps you could grab a book and relax by the fire."

I shot her a look. She knew I wouldn't sit and relax—not before I saw for myself how he fared.

She sighed long and loudly.

"You're asking for whatever trouble befalls you, girl."

"My favorite," I said as I smirked.

Evelyn waved her hand, dismissing me and my antics. I donned my coat and buttoned up against the cold.

The day was late, and the afternoon sun glistened blindingly against the white snow that was smudged with red and brown. There were tracks leading away from the chaos, and I itched to follow them to see how many dragons were in Whalen's possession.

Looking around, I noticed no one and followed the insane urge toward imminent doom. If the dragons didn't get me, it would surely be Whalen who did.

But something had changed since my parents' death. After I relinquished the burden of my birthright, a degree of reckless abandon came with my rediscovered freedom. It lifted a weight from my shoulders.

And ripped a hole in my soul. I'd gladly take my parents back in favor of losing my freedom again. As it was, I wouldn't waste the refreshing lightness that came with the loss of my queenly duties.

Part of me knew it was a big reason for my recent bout of death wishes. I had little left to live for. Even the prospect of Oisin, of fulfilling our parents' wishes and saving my people, had begun to wane.

Before, I had clung to it like a lifeline. Now it chafed, the final shackle preventing me from being blissfully unattached to anyone and anything.

So possibly I followed those tracks to run further from my remaining responsibilities. Or closer to my ultimate freedom—death's sweet embrace.

Who knew, really?

But I kept following the muddy tracks in the snow as they wended their way through the field and skirted the woods until I heard them. Not an overly loud noise, as if they were all complacent about being chained to trees and monitored by men.

The men didn't notice my approach. It seemed the late afternoon was the time for rest in between meals, the evidence of which stained the snow in a massacre of red in front of each dragon, and before preparations for the night.

As I counted the beasts, I noticed they were generally relaxed. Only the sound of their loud breathing was evident among the occasional rustle of wings.

That's when I noticed the dragon from the night before and him me.

I didn't have a chance to observe him last night, but now as we locked eyes, I could see the calculating gleam lying there. Easily the largest of the dozen or so, he was also the darkest. The forest green of his scales was deceptive against the trees, which I imagined was the point.

He moved, getting into a crouch that had me on alert. His eyes were a similar shade of green, like ivy, and they watched me earnestly.

I froze in place, not daring to move, hardly breathing as I continued to look at the creatures. Keeping an eye on the monster dragon, I inspected the others.

Though smaller, they couldn't be considered tiny, each as large as or bigger than the barn. Their colors varied, but they were all suited to camouflage either in the sky or the mountains. One was as big as the green one but was as milky white as a cloud.

A growl rumbled nearby, much closer to me than the dragons were, and I jumped out of my skin at the sudden noise. I whipped my head in the direction it came from, half expecting to be burned alive.

More like flayed alive.

Whalen stood there, eyes yellow, another growl rumbling in his chest. An inhuman noise.

He prowled toward me, covering the ground quickly with his long strides. I refused to balk, not allowing a flinch or a cringe to give him any satis-faction.

He stopped a couple inches from me, my chest brushing against the furs he wore and his mouth hovering above mine as he met my eyes with an intensity I'd never seen before. I matched his look with one of my own, willing fire into it. He wouldn't intimidate me.

"What don't you understand, woman?"

"I could ask you the same thing," I challenged, feeling the sneer on my face with a touch of delirious joy.

"And what exactly is it that I don't seem to grasp? That you're hell-bent on destroying yourself no matter the collateral damage? Oh, I get that quite well."

Lightning struck my stomach, the pain a physical reaction. He felt the words land true; I saw it in the surprise in his eyes, the truth hitting him at the same time—not that I was about to back down, though.

"That no one is in control of me but me," I said, willing my vehemence into my voice.

The storm clouds in his eyes cleared some, but he didn't move back, didn't lose the sneer. Neither did I. Instead, we stood there, locked in a silent battle, neither gaining an inch.

"I'm in charge of your safety and the safety of

the men and women here. And you seem determined to interfere with me doing so."

"I'm not interested in hindering your ability to protect anyone. Though I don't recall anyone ever putting you in charge...."

"Those men," he said, pointing toward the men on guard whose attention was beginning to turn our way, "they follow me. If you don't want to, you are welcome to leave."

He knew he had me. Where was I going to go? The weather was too cold yet to travel, and a woman traveling alone to no one knew where was hardly feasible. Not if I wanted to live.

I didn't say any of that, only gritted my teeth in consternation.

"I was looking for my escort," I said, the closest I was willing to go toward acquiescence.

"Of course you are, Emer," he said, grabbing my arm and hurtling me alongside him.

He half dragged me to the stream, his face stony. I refused to say anything, but I let him tow me along, stunned by his words. I hadn't meant to endanger anyone else, though that was exactly what I did last night. Joseph would bear the scars of my hasty decisions for the rest of his life. And here I was, doing it again.

But it wasn't that I was trying to destroy myself —or was it? I knew I was brash, and had maybe become more so since my parents' death, but perhaps actions and consequences weren't at the forefront of my mind. Though I'd been chasing danger with reckless abandon, was I truly prepared to perish by my own hand?

He finally stopped and let me go to stomp away from me. I saw Joseph then, and him us, his face inquisitive.

I couldn't hear what Whalen said to him. I simply watched the lines of aggression roll off the White Wolf in waves, his men looking on curiously. Joseph just nodded, waiting until he was dismissed before making his way to me, still standing numbly where Whalen had deposited me.

His expression as he approached was not one of reproach. He seemed mildly concerned and a little amused. I was livid but perhaps also a little mollified, the ire leeching from me—at least enough to quell my desire for the fight spoiling inside me. Maybe later, when we weren't in public and it would cause a scene.

The years of high-society training tempered me even as it angered me, that same control I had referred to coming back to rear its ugly head. *Sit up straight, don't speak out of turn, and obey."* I was raised to be a good wife to a man of my station, and though I always chafed at the restrictions, I had rarely broken free from them.

Something about Whalen seemed to always make me cross the line. Not that I normally backed down from a fight, but I hardly provoked one. What I did now was ask for it, begging Whalen to react unfairly.

Except he didn't, not really. I could sit in righteous indignation at having a babysitter, but I'd brought it on myself.

Whalen looked at me all the while Joseph crossed the distance between us. His face was unreadable, but the tension in his shoulders spoke volumes. I was strangely crushed by his disapproval, another lingering effect of my upbringing.

I hated to cede control, but I hated even more to put people at risk and additional pressure on Whalen.

Oh heavens, I was worried about our captor's feelings.

While gazing at him another moment, it hit me —he'd called me Emer. Damn, what did that even signify?

I looked too long, making Joseph frown. Unsure of whether anyone should know yet, I shook my head. If Whalen was privy to that information and chose to sit on it, then so could I. However, it was still concerning. Knowing my name was one thing, but what else did he know? I'd have to wheedle more information out of him first before I knew how to address that.

The question was, what did he have to gain?

Maybe he was trying to win me over so he could what, steal my land? He already did.

But how did he figure it out? I wouldn't say I was a superb maid, but I was passable, at least. Knowing my true identity opened up a world of complexities to our interactions to this point. The White Wolf would have the ability to build an army much larger than his already sizable one with the money he would inherit from my hand in marriage, for one.

Joseph had made it to me, and I tried to seem angered or frustrated—any of the normal responses to being carted around like a rag doll. I must have failed, because his frown deepened.

"Hello, chaperone," I said offhandedly.

"Bodyguard more than anything. I'm to not leave your side, come hell or high water."

"Were those his instructions, then?" I asked, resigned.

"Don't be so excited to have my company."

"You know well enough that it has nothing to do with you."

He smiled, a mischievous thing. I was glad for it because my tenacity could be off-putting to some.

"How are you feeling? That's why I came out here," I asked, as it was partially the truth and furthermore to change the subject from Whalen, who still brooded at the edge of the woods with his men, looking at me half as much as I was at him.

Emer. The mention of my name was making me feel spacey—the truth of me so far removed from the reality I'd been living.

Joseph had answered my query, but I hadn't truly listened, the noise sounding far away and unfamiliar. They finally hit me seconds after they were spoken.

"Stiff, but I'll be fine" was what he'd uttered.

I clearly took too long to answer, though, because then he echoed my previous words emphatically.

"How are *you* feeling?"

"Fine," I lied. "Tired is all."

A believable lie, though, and one he accepted

willingly. We'd been up the better part of the night, and though I had slept, it wasn't a normal night.

"Aye, that I am too," he said, and he looked it. A glossiness coated his eyes, and they were puffy from lack of sleep.

Guilt swept over me again, as I had planned on making him adventure with me despite Whalen's irritation. But the man deserved to rest.

"We can go inside, then. Are you hungry?"

"I am at your service," he said with a wink.

"You don't need to do that with me. You're hungry, then?" I repeated.

He smirked in acquiescence and relief.

"Famished," he admitted.

"Come, then. Let's eat," I told him.

Though I had only finished eating, I should still stomach more. Thrown off by the late night, my body needed to pack in the calories it had missed today. I wouldn't say I was hungry, but for Joseph, I would try.

The sun had already begun its descent, the winter months making nights stretch on forever. The creeping darkness was oddly comforting, suiting the black mood that still clung to me, made worse by Whalen's confirmation of my fears.

He hadn't killed me yet, which was a good sign.

Maybe he didn't want to eliminate the competition. Or worse, Oisin would be his true nemesis, as his claim on me would mean Whalen had no chance. But with Joseph already exposed, it ratcheted my anxiety up higher. Oisin could be found out at any moment, and who knew how Whalen would respond.

Unless his plan had already been in play. Perhaps that was why he had been so *attentive* lately.

We made it to the house to find Evelyn bustling around the kitchen, keeping herself busy. She brightened as she noticed us.

They exchanged pleasantries, and food was placed in front of us, but I hardly had the attention for it. I was swirling in my own head again, trying to piece together the events of the last few weeks. It wasn't until the subject of bed came up that I was stolen from my reverie.

"I was explicitly told to never let her out of my sight," Joseph said, giving me a roguish grin so out of character from any I had seen before from him.

"Good. I'll send up the spare pillows, blankets, and cot for you," Evelyn said, smiling herself.

"Wait, wait, wait. You don't mean to sleep in my bedroom, do you?" I asked, astounded.

"Where else would he sleep if he's to keep you in check? I might put some bells on the door, too, just in case you're a heavy sleeper, Joseph," Evelyn said with wicked mischief in her eyes.

She was enjoying this.

"And what if I oppose?" I demanded vehemently.

"I would bring it up with the boss," Joseph replied a little too flippantly.

Weren't they supposed to be enemies too? Or was this one of those times that opposing companies unite for a mutual cause?

"No, thanks. I'll manage," I said, my ego chafing at the options.

Putting up with Joseph at night was better than arguing with Whalen over my rights. I didn't relish acquiescing, but keeping Joseph close meant we could collaborate on how to get out of this situation. Didn't Whalen realize that?

I was trying to work out his ulterior motive while they sent men to reorganize my room for company. I was coming up blank. There was no advantage I could see except to keep his enemies close. And we would be intimately close to Whalen at night, sharing a wall with him.

If I was being honest with myself, I was grateful

for Joseph's intrusion for that reason alone. Probably Whalen was too.

Simply remembering him in my bedroom this morning elicited a visceral response from me, one that had my cheeks flaming at the direction of my thoughts as if I'd said them out loud. The fear escalated when I noticed Evelyn and Joseph staring at me expectantly.

"What?" I asked, my breath a little too short.

"Ready?" Joseph asked, eyes sparkling, and my worries became something altogether different.

I hoped Joseph didn't think my reaction was in response to him. Now I was cursing Whalen for real. At least I didn't think I'd said my thoughts out loud, but they seemed to have been broadcast regardless.

"Sure," I said, grateful to at least escape Evelyn's searching gaze as she put pieces of the puzzle together herself.

I rolled my eyes at her, and she smirked.

"Have a good night, you two." She winked at me, and I narrowed my eyes in disapproval. She could be a piece of work when she wanted to be.

Her tinkling laugh followed us out of the kitchen, and Joseph chuckled as he trailed in my wake. I turned and gave him a withering glare, but it only made him laugh more.

I didn't know what they found so entertaining. My being on house arrest was a gross overuse of Whalen's powers. One I intended to exploit.

"Wait, shouldn't we change your bandages?" I asked suddenly.

If I was going to use him to get back at Whalen, the least I could do was make sure he was in good shape before we did so.

"No, I'm fine—truly. Thank you," he said gently, a curious look on his face.

"What?" I questioned.

He shook his head, opening my bedroom door for me. The cot took up the floor, leaving only inches for walking between the beds, but it was enough.

"Get comfortable. I'll wait out here," he said, then closed the door behind me.

*So much for not letting me out of his sight.*

I would have made a remark, but truthfully, I was ready to get into something more comfortable. And I wouldn't mind doing it without a strange man watching me.

I made quick work of it and then called out to Joseph, giving him the all clear to come in.

"I'm going to use the bathroom," I told him, and the face he made had me amending, "I'll be right out, I promise."

He was still waiting in the hallway when I emerged from the bathroom. I rolled my eyes.

"You're taking this too seriously."

"Maybe you're not taking it seriously enough."

"The White Wolf turned you around, didn't he?"

"We have an understanding," he said cryptically.

"Care to divulge?"

"Not particularly." He yawned exaggeratedly.

Guilt ran through me. He was no doubt exhausted after last night. I had the benefit of sleeping in half the day; I wasn't sure he had the same privilege. Hopefully, now that he was stuck with me, I could force him to get more rest to heal better.

It was a little awkward settling in bed so close to Joseph's cot, but he made it as comfortable as possible. The worst part was that I wasn't tired. I lay there with my eyes closed and tried to relax as thoughts swirled around.

A fruitless effort.

I grew more agitated as time marched on. Eventually, the sound of Joseph's even breathing reached me, though instead of relaxing me, it made me more frustrated. I would rather be tired, but it wasn't happening.

Time was simultaneously racing toward dawn

and not moving at all as I gave up and stared at the ceiling lit by the moon's reflection off the snow. It created a cozy feeling that I was growing resentful of as comfort evaded me.

Eventually, I could no longer bear the incessant tossing and turning and decided to creep out of the bedroom in an effort to shake this restlessness.

Joseph didn't move as I inched my way out of bed and past him. I had no intentions of going outside or doing anything that would get him in trouble, so leaving him behind was fine. Whalen's method was effective, I thought irritably. Even if I could sneak past Joseph, my fear of retribution was stronger regarding him than for myself. I had little doubt that the White Wolf planned on utilizing leverage against me.

I held my breath as I opened the door, moving so slowly, it took a lifetime to get the door open enough that I could slink through. Sneaking out without waking my parents was practice I was used to. Sadness washed over me at the thought, but I blocked it out, burying the emotion like I did time and again. It was a useless effort, grieving. It felt vast as an ocean. If I succumbed to the feeling, I would surely drown.

So I suffocated it further with every inch I got

away from my bedroom, focusing on the task ahead. Seeking the peace of mind that existed solely at night, when the only living creatures to share my energy with were other loners.

Relief washed over me the minute I reached the kitchen window and looked out over the quiet snow. I hadn't realized I'd been clenching my jaw until it released, and I stretched it to reduce the tension.

"You're incorrigible," a deep voice said behind me, and I squeaked in surprise, whirling around to see Whalen at the entrance of the kitchen.

"You scared the daylights out of me," I admonished, one hand on my rapidly beating heart.

"Now you know the feeling," he said with a raised eyebrow.

I let that sink in as I calmed my breath, trying to look away from him. He was shirtless with his pants slung low on his waist, as if he'd thrown them on to race after me. Desire yawned awake in me, and I found myself biting my lip. I went back to clenching my jaw instead before I looked back up at him, trying to get a grip on my hormones.

I failed.

"As if," I said irritably.

"As if what?" he retorted smoothly, his usual growl honeyed in his near whisper.

"I could frighten you that way." I found it hard to imagine he was frightened of anything.

He didn't answer immediately, only looked at me with dark eyes.

"I'm as surprised as you," he said eventually, his gaze searing me in its intensity.

I would look away if I could.

"Surprised?" I whispered, cursing my breathlessness.

He focused on my mouth then, and I realized I was biting my lip again. I released it immediately, only to notice how dry my mouth had gone.

Electricity swamped the air between us as he crossed the room quietly. I felt like one of the deer he hunted, caught between fight or flight.

In the end, I froze, captivated by his eyes as they held mine and gleamed in the light from the window. They weren't quite yellow this time but amber, burning with a glow I'd never seen before.

He stopped mere inches from me, my back against the sink. I clenched its edge to keep from reaching out to him to trace my fingers over his bare chest. My hormones were on a rampage now, tearing through me like lightning, making me ache for him in a way I'd never experienced before—at least not this strongly. It was a heady feeling that short-circuited my brain.

"Very" was all he said, leaning down until his mouth hovered over mine, our breaths mingling.

I was panting now, so lost in my need for him that I couldn't care less. Especially not when he was equally lost, his muscular pecs heaving with the force of his breathing, abs showing with every exhale.

The last of my resolve melted when he gripped my hips, the strength in his hold grounding me as much as it flew me to the moon. He seemed to notice the shift because when the walls finally crumbled, he lowered his lips to meet mine.

Just the briefest contact, a brush of his mouth on mine—the first kiss. The gasp that erupted from me was all the invitation he needed before he kissed me again, firmer this time, pulling me closer as he pushed his body against mine.

I dragged him closer still, digging my fingers into the muscles in his lower back, and I groaned at the strong columns flanking his spine. Encouraged by my moan, he deepened the kiss further, his tongue reaching out to caress my lips.

Then he was lifting me by my waist to rest my ass on the edge of the sink. I grabbed onto his shoulders. Much to my delight, they were even more massive than they looked, especially without clothing.

My nightgown rode up my hips as he pressed his into them, the thin material of my underwear the only thing separating my skin from his. He roughly pulled me closer as he continued to consume my every breath and whimper.

It was his hand on my bare thigh that undid me. I was so close to begging him to take me on the kitchen table when it hit me.

Emer.

"You said my name," I gasped between kisses.

"Said what?" he asked, his voice gravelly, going to kiss me again.

I put a hand on his chest, stopping his momentum, and beneath the haze of desire, there was concern in his eyes.

Damn it but I wanted to wrap my legs around him.

But this was too important.

"My real name," I said, breath still uneven.

"Emer," he groaned, eyes locked on my lips.

"How did you know?" I asked, shoving again as he tried to close the distance that was killing both of us.

He leaned in then, easily passing my feeble defense. Only he didn't kiss me the way I thought he would. Instead, he angled his head sideways, his nose grazing my neck from my shoulder to my ear as he inhaled deeply.

"You can change your name and cut your beautiful hair, darling, but you can't change your scent," he whispered in my ear before biting delicately at the lobe, sending liquid fire straight to my core.

I caved slightly, hooking my legs around his hips and squeezing him closer with my thighs. His deep chuckle broke the spell a little.

"How?"

"My senses are heightened even in human form. Your scent is everywhere in this house, and it's concentrated in your bedroom. The first time I met you, I knew."

"But you let me keep pretending. Why? How did you know who I was?"

"Who you *are*," he emphasized. "Because you're not the only royalty in the room," he replied, letting that sink in a moment. "I let you pretend because you needed to."

"What do you mean?"

"My scent isn't limited to who you are. I can also detect emotions. Not through smell alone—I can also hear how fast or slow your heart beats as well as perceive certain pheromones," he said with a sheepish grin.

I felt the blush instantly as it took over my whole body. This whole time, he'd known every indecent thought I'd had about him.

"Can you elaborate on the last one?" I asked, looking at him through my long lashes.

The grin he gave me was nothing short of predatory. I couldn't stop the primal reaction if I wanted to. The haze of desire made me forget what we were talking about by the time he answered.

"Even if I couldn't smell a thing, there is no mistaking the way you look at me," he said, his voice an octave lower again.

Damn it.

Even as his words pulled me in, I was reminded of how many women looked at him that way. I was certain I was not the first to be smitten by the infamous White Wolf, only to be cast aside after he'd gotten his fill.

Then I remembered.

He wouldn't use me only for my body but for my name and titles too. The ones that were Oisin's by right as his betrothed. He would get this manor, the farmlands surrounding it, and every cent to my name if he married me. And who knew what he would use it for? Though I had a semblance of trust in him, that might be exactly what he wanted.

Regret thundered through me at the thought of Oisin, but I didn't have time for that now. Right now I had to get back upstairs—*alone.*

"Like my next conquest?" I inquired, trying to flip the dynamic on its head, the used becoming the user.

"Is that what I am?"

"Oh, aye," I said mockingly, hopping off the sink ledge after pushing him farther away. "You were going to be, but I've changed my mind."

"You would prefer the bloodsucker to me?" he quipped, a little more offended than I was prepared for.

I blinked as I evaluated his words.

"Bloodsucker?" I questioned.

"I told you much more was happening than you realized. Right, Joseph?" he asked with a sneer.

"Joseph?" He wasn't in the room.

But from the shadows in the hallway, a figure emerged. A bit of a reticent one, if I wasn't mistaken.

"Correct, sir," he said, inclining his head in respect toward Whalen.

His nod set my blood boiling, and I knew it made

me a hypocrite. I'd just been kissing the man, after all.

"What did you think, that I put your friend in charge of you to make you happy?"

I didn't say anything, especially not given the snarky attitude with which he delivered this news. Instead, I ground my teeth and waited for him to elaborate. If dragons and those like Whalen, the púca, were real, I didn't see why the Abhartach wouldn't be, but again, it begged the question of why?

It dawned on me then—he'd put a vampire in my bedroom to watch over me while I slept!

"I see the wheels turning in your pretty head, darling, but don't worry—he's not after *your* blood. And besides, they have all those rules about entering and all that, so when I invited him into your bedroom, I made sure to mention there would be no drinking anyone's blood here, not unless they expressly gave him permission themselves. About which, as the current ruler of this clan at the moment, I have the final say."

"Since when were you the ruler, if you know who I am?"

"I am since I took the helm, the one you seemingly abdicated. If you'd like it back, I'd be happy to fight you for it," he said with a wink before continuing. "But alas, Joseph is uniquely situated to watch you perpetually, seeing as he's not in need of sleep any time in the next millennia. And he has spectacular hearing and vision, so good luck escaping him now that I've put him on your tail."

"Well, good thing I don't have to escape him—I only have to escape *you*," I said a bit angrily.

To Joseph's credit, he seemed quite apologetic, but ample lore supported Whalen's claims. There were loopholes in inviting vampires into your home, if you knew enough to exploit them. My father had often told me the stories in his fanatical way.

Or at least I'd always thought of it that way. Perhaps he'd been onto something the whole time.

*What if he knew all along?*

The thought unnerved me enough that a chill finally worked its way down my spine, making me react in a way these revelations couldn't. How much had my parents known about this Otherworld?

I started looking at Joseph, picking him apart. His dark complexion was perhaps waxier than was natural, but he also had been hiding in the cellar beneath the barn for weeks with Oisin and the other men. After a rather brutal battle, I might add. Maybe I had expected his pallor to be sickly?

His mouth was closed, so I couldn't see the fangs or any indication there were any. But his eyes were sharp—unnervingly so.

I had chalked it up to his experience on the battlefield, but what if that was the difference?

He moved then, so fast I didn't realize he was doing it. He stood directly in front of me now, smiling fully at me with his teeth on display—or should I say fangs? Because those were undoubtedly elongated canines that grew even as I watched, desperately grasping the counter behind me, though I didn't remember doing it.

That was when I rehashed the events from the night before. How could Joseph have feasibly gotten to me before the dragon? The only way was if he'd been following me the whole time, but I didn't remember hearing or seeing him.

Though I supposed I wouldn't have. But maybe it had been his vampiric speed all along. I had been too flustered to think of it.

"But wait...," I said, trailing off as Joseph went back to a good soldier stance, as if he were responding to cues I wasn't privy to.

"Yes, he ran to intercept the dragon last night," Whalen answered for me.

Apparently, I was the only one incapable of reading minds, then.

"Well, then, why didn't you stop me in the first place?" I asked, a bit baffled.

"I'd hoped you'd continue on your way, when both you and the dragon were unaware of each other. Dragons are most vulnerable, and irritable, when they're eating. They don't pay much attention to anything outside of food when it's in front of them. The only trouble is if they see you," Joseph answered, his soothing voice such a stark contrast to my keening one.

I made a mental note to try to play it cool from this point forward.

"Your hope was that I'd walk on by?"

"It failed, clearly," Whalen interjected, and I shot him daggers.

"You were outside in the sun, though," I said, my mind racing through the legends, trying to put logic to the fantasy I found myself living. I thought I'd found the loophole at last, a way out of Whalen's ridiculous power struggle with me.

"It doesn't affect them as we've always been wont to believe. Only, similar to wolves, they are superior hunters at night," Whalen chimed in smugly.

But Oisin, did he know?

I tried desperately looking at Joseph, praying he could read the thought in my head. But again the damn man in front of me, the one who looked so sexy in his element right now, was the one who answered.

"You didn't think your poultice was so superior that Oisin was all but healed the next day, did you?"

Finally, my stomach plummeted. All my cards laid bare, like the sheep that wandered into the lion's den—or I supposed the wolf's den.

"He was dying. There's no doubt about it. But hiding with a vampire has its benefits if they aren't planning on draining you dry."

Wait, he couldn't be saying what I thought he was, was he?

"Oisin's not... he's not... he wasn't," I said, fumbling for words.

"Oh yes, he is, sweetheart. But we're all full of surprises here, aren't we?" Whalen asked cryptically.

I didn't know what he meant by that, so I squinted in a universal look of *What the hell are you talking about?*

"You truly don't know, then, *Emer*?"

"What, that I hid my identity?"

"Well, Joseph, if we aren't full of secrets as well as surprises. Did you not stop to wonder why your father taught you quite so much?"

"Well, I'm heir, or I was," I said confusedly.

"What woman do you know who is as knowledgeable as yourself?"

I tried thinking of the other women of my status I knew. Most were more involved in gossip than anything of meaning, a fact that kept us divided. My father had always reminded me to behave more like them, though, much to my chagrin. Coming up empty, I merely shrugged.

"He wasn't preparing you to be an heir alone. He was readying you to be a priestess, as he was a priest."

"He wasn't a priest," I said, perplexed.

We had some of them come through our village, men who never married and were devoted to God, whom they taught us about. Some people began following their religion, something my father resisted, keeping to our traditions.

"Not like those men but a priest of old. The men and women the legends tell us about."

"A Druid, you mean?" I asked, a little baffled. We didn't have Druids. They weren't real.

He raised an eyebrow at me, the gesture dripping with his brand of egotism. I didn't say anything at first, letting his words sink in. If the other creatures we had only ever heard legends about were real, I didn't see why Druids couldn't be as well.

"But why?" I asked at last, the only question that mattered.

"He knew we were going to need you."

"NEED ME FOR WHAT?"

How could I be a priestess? All I had were stories. What was I going to do, bore people to death? In the legends, Druids were powerful healers, seers, and magic wielders. I was capable enough at healing, but I knew no spells, and I couldn't see the future. If I could, I wouldn't be so mind-boggled at the moment.

I had expected Whalen to answer, but it was Joseph's soft tenor that rang out.

"It's been centuries since I've seen more of my kind. There would be the occasional one in my travels, but most were, like myself, made when the world was new and magic was a wild untamed thing.

"Then, we could travel between realms without fear, and we would prey on humans in their world. All kinds of creatures did. But for as many who preyed on them, there were plenty more who traded with them—knowledge, supplies, and DNA.

"Until there came a time that the human world had grown strong—potentially stronger than ours. Some bore children with the humans, and vice versa, celebrating the uniting of our two worlds. Many more protested, claiming inferiority, that it was a disgrace to treat humans as equals.

"Dagda, the All-Father, had closed the portals between realms, forbidding the Fae world from interacting with the humans. He'd found a way to prevent war, both internal and external, knowing he couldn't wage a war on both fronts.

"The magic dimmed then, and supernatural beings found ways to manage on their own. For my kind, the transition was more difficult. Where humans were perfect prey, and there were plenty, the beings in the Otherworld were keener and more difficult to hunt.

"Many were lost, and few adapted like we did and learned to survive. But surviving was not thriving. We didn't die, but there weren't new Abhartach being created, and the survivors dwindled.

"But now, I come across more all the time. Donal, who you met with Oisin, has been traveling with me for a year or a little more. I changed Oisin, lest he be lost for good, an ability I haven't been able to manage since before the worlds were divided.

"Púca, like Whalen, were all but extinct, becoming ordinary, no better than a human. But latent genes in their lineage have been showing up more and more, none more famously than in the White Wolf himself.

"Something is stirring up the magic—or someone. Dagda has been preparing, though for what, we can't say. We came here on the tails of bandits, thieves who were relishing in the chaos being created and heading to join an army that's supposed to be a faction opposing Dagda and his rules.

"The Queen of Elphame is at the helm of this militia, enacting her long-awaited stand against the status quo. Those men were unruly, though—untrained. If we had caught up to them before they made it here, we could have disbanded them. We are forever in your debt because of our failure."

I didn't say anything. It wasn't their fault what happened. And our clan should have been able to handle an untrained force. I still wondered why we failed.

At my silence, he continued.

"We believe you may prove vital in the days to come. While we're unsure of what to anticipate, Druids have always served as a force for good against evil. So we rushed here to help and to save you if we could," he finished at last.

"But why me? Aren't there more like me? Ones who actually know what they're doing?"

"There are others, but they are few and far between. And they're often kept secret until they're ready to be of help. Your father was one, and rumor had it you had the connection," Whalen said, his tone more somber than I was used to.

"Connection?"

"Aye. Being a Druid involves more than the physical. It's the spiritual as well, like the connection to other realms or speaking to our ancestors."

"Speaking to them?" I whispered.

"Speaking to them, aye," Whalen said softly, his eyes shining with understanding.

"But I don't know how," I protested.

"I know, darling, but we have a plan."

I glared at him. I didn't appreciate the sweet nothings while I was waiting impatiently for him to continue.

"There's a rumor in the north of an ancient and powerful Druid. We hope he may be able to help."

"Well, why not go straight to him and skip me altogether?"

They did the classic exchange of looks, neither of them wanting to offer up whatever information they both had.

Finally Whalen spoke up.

"He's not particularly fond of me. Nor Joseph, as I understand it, or my other men by proxy. But you, who are so emphatically against me," he said with a raised eyebrow and a smirk, "might be able to entreat him."

"To do what, exactly?"

"Undermine the queen, usurp her power, prevent a war," he said nonchalantly.

"Me?"

"Well, I suppose it would be you and Amergin or some combination of people."

"War, you said?"

My mind was melting from information overload. I kept staring at Joseph, trying to see the differences in his features. Did he stand too still? Were his eyes too sharp?

"Yes, war. The Underworld has long chafed against Dagda's reign. The darker creatures of our realm were hit the hardest by cutting off our worlds, since they preyed on many of the weaker humans and Fae. It's been a slow process, but they may have the strength to rise up now. Unless we can help prevent it before it ever gets to that point."

"That sounds well and good, but what's in it for you? Why does it matter so much?"

His gaze darkened then, and if I wasn't mistaken, a flash of yellow glinted in the dim light. Joseph went impossibly stiller, as if he didn't even draw a breath.

"We all have our motivations," he said simply.

He wouldn't give me an answer. The atmosphere in the room hung thick and heavy now, and I suddenly wanted nothing more than to escape back to my room. Until I remembered I would be sleeping next to Joseph, who, vow or not, I was a touch more anxious to be so vulnerable next to. Luckily, Whalen seemed to want out of this conversation as much as I did.

"If you're not about to bolt out the door and make a run for it, I'd like to get back to bed," he said.

Damn my hormones again. The mention of him in bed had me reliving the feeling of his hands on my hips, his mouth on mine, the hardness of his muscles as they pressed against me. I valiantly tried to keep my breathing even and my heart rate down, but the looks on their faces told me I had failed. So I bolted.

"Bed, then," I said, whisking past them before either could utter a retort.

I made sure not to touch Whalen in my hasty retreat, but before I could pass him, he threw out an arm to wrap around my waist. Leaning down, he whispered to me close enough that his scruff tickled the shell, sending shivers to my core.

"You could join me if you'd feel safer," he said, and I had to look into his eyes to check, but the offer was sincere despite the tension between us.

The offer did funny things to my heart that I tried to ignore, but truthfully, I was melting. However, the feel of his strong arm around me, holding my waist tenderly but surely, told me it would be impossible to sleep next to him.

At least not before slaking my desire for him.

I was biting my lip again, and I released it the minute I came out of my daze. The temptation was enticing.

But I still wasn't sure how much I trusted him. And I hated it.

"It's okay. I trust Joseph. Thank you, though," I said softly, and I was pretty sure I saw disappointment in his eyes, but the look was gone as quickly as it came. I could see him warring with a response, but in the end, he just released me with a nod.

"All right, then. Good night," he said, a gentle smile on his face that didn't reach his eyes.

"Good night," I muttered, despair rocketing through me.

Had I chosen the wrong words? Perhaps a simple "No, thank you" would have sufficed. But I'd told the truth. I did trust Joseph. Whalen I was uncertain about, a fact I made abundantly clear with my choice of wording.

I was kicking myself the whole way up the stairs, Joseph on my heels. The silence was palpable, but no sound came from the Abhartach. A shiver ran down my spine, the sensation of being watched—or rather, stalked—rampaging through me.

"I'm sorry," Joseph muttered when we made it to my room.

"What for?" I asked sincerely. The creepy feeling was gone now that he wasn't behind me anymore, and I felt a little guilty for having been uncomfortable at all.

"That I scare you now," he said, his soft voice a melody. It was so flowing that I could feel the pull toward him, undoubtedly a good trick for a vampire to lure in their prey.

"You don't scare me," I said automatically, and he didn't. I was a little more cautious now, though.

"I do, and I should." His voice held a note of anger in it that had me examining him more closely. "But I wanted you to know I don't hunt your kind."

"Druids, you mean?"

"I don't hunt humans or lesser Fae."

"Well, who *do* you hunt?"

"I'll either hunt animals or prey I think deserves it," he said cryptically.

"Deserves it?" I questioned.

"I suppose I have to amend my previous statement. If there's a human or lesser Fae who prefers to prey on the weak themselves or is otherwise morally unsound, I may hunt them. Though generally, it's only animals I will drink from."

"Do you kill them?" I didn't know if it mattered much, but I was curious.

He seemed pleased with my question, as if most people he explained this to always assumed he did.

"Not animals, at least."

"But humans?"

"That is on a case-by-case basis. If I think they

would benefit society by ceasing to exist, then I believe them to be forfeit already."

"And you think you know best? Determining who lives and who dies?" I asked a little skeptically. I wasn't certain I'd feel comfortable with a similar level of power.

"I think it's survival of the fittest. There have been occasions when I was wrong on both ends— taking a life I had misjudged and saving one I ought not to have. In both instances, I still proved superior, and perhaps there is a design greater than you or I could begin to fathom. I am merely the instrument of the Fates."

"You think the Morrigan has anything to say about it?"

"I think if I ever get to Tech Duinn, I suppose I'll find out what she thought," he said ruefully.

"How does a vampire land in the afterlife?"

"Painfully," he said with a wry smile.

He wasn't going to reveal all his tricks to me, just in case. I understood it. I wouldn't offer up my weaknesses if I could help it.

"When do you... feed?" I asked, fumbling for the right word.

"Not as often as you, but it depends on the size of the prey and how much blood I'm able to obtain.

A bear can last me a month, but smaller prey only a week or so."

"So, when did you last eat?" I asked, trying to hide the slight tingle of fear down my spine.

He chuckled, giving me a smirk. I suppose I hadn't hidden my fear well enough.

"I'm not hungry right now, don't worry," he said.

I tried to be content with that answer. But truthfully, I was too worried about what or whom he ate to be satisfied.

He must have sensed my discomfort, because after a few beats, he continued.

"The White Wolf caught a few animals lately, didn't he?"

"Yes," I said, waiting for him to complete the thought.

"I drained them. Whalen let me and Donal have them first," he explained with a raised eyebrow.

"Oh," I said, a little embarrassed and a lot more relieved. I don't know why it mattered, but the idea that he could feed on anyone he wanted unnerved me. Friends and family, children, pets. And he blended right in—there was no way to tell him apart from another human.

"Do all of your kind...?"

"No," he said, catching my train of thought. "Most of my kind primarily feed off humans. The others with me are like me, if that's your next question."

"Yes, actually. Thank you," I said softly.

He made a noise deep in his throat, a cross between amusement and acknowledgment. I tried to look away from him, but I couldn't stop examining the differences I could see. There weren't a ton.

"I can sleep in the other room, if you'd rather," he offered gently.

I mulled it over. Screw politeness when it came to sleep. Could I close my eyes if I were next to a vampire?

But on Joseph's face, there was nothing but patience and kindness. And a shrewdness shining in his dark eyes told me he could already read my answer on my face.

"It's fine, really," I said, and I meant it. I did trust Joseph, even if I had my reservations.

"If you change your mind, say so, okay?" he asked, patting my hand.

"I will," I said, biting my lip.

He looked at me like he could see the thoughts still swirling in my head.

"Yes?"

"Do you genuinely think I serve a purpose in this *thing*?" I asked, unsure of what to call it.

"I do, as a matter of fact. Do you remember the wars that put Dagda in power years ago?"

"I mean, I know of them," I said. I was too young to have been alive to witness the war.

"They say wars are won by war councils, not on the battlefield. This Druid we're going to meet was crucial to turning the tide and placing Dagda on the throne. We're hoping he will prove key to keeping him on it this time. The woman who would have him replaced is reckless and cruel. She would have the Underworld reign freely, killing and using whomever they pleased, which is quite like the days before Dagda separated them. But if dragons cause this much damage, imagine what other monsters lurk in the darkness that she would unleash. We're keen on maintaining the status quo."

"But why me? Why not go to him? Isn't this what he wants too?"

"He wants nothing to do with it this time."

"So, if he wants nothing to do with the war and even less to do with Whalen, what makes you think he'll work with me at all?"

"Truthfully, we don't know this will work.

However, we do think he won't be able to resist you," he said, and I cocked an eyebrow.

"So, I'm supposed to seduce him?" I asked, a little outraged.

He smiled, and it was a cunning one. I was more than a little surprised by that. Joseph hadn't shown any of the wickedness that I was so accustomed to from Whalen. It was gone in a flash, though, the same placid look returning to his face. But it had my antennae up.

"We hope you don't, and I can't imagine it would work even if you tried. Whalen has a history with Amergin, as do I, and we're working off a theory."

"Which is?" I demanded, a little exasperated at the cat-and-mouse game.

"To put it succinctly, you both have shared trauma. We think it will make it impossible for him to deny you."

"You're planning on using his trauma against him?" I hardly thought it was a viable plan.

"It does sound terrible when you put it that way. It's a necessary evil, or so we've concluded."

I merely looked at him with my best exasperated expression. If he was going to explain things, he might as well do it thoroughly.

"All right, then. If the Fates are like the seers, the Druids manipulate the magic, making the Fates' visions a reality. Amergin was pivotal in the wars that seated Dagda on the throne, but we never said that was his goal.

"In truth, Amergin was one of the rebel leaders, launching the assault against the Tuatha de Danann in revenge for his great-uncle Ith, who was killed by the three kings of the time. This led to a peace treaty in which the queens of the Tuatha de Danann granted Amergin and his brothers the right to settle on the land as long as they named the land for each of the queens. The catch was that they first had to defeat the kings in battle.

"Amergin acted as the judge, setting the rules for engagement. While his side, the Milesians, went behind a magical boundary to begin the battle, the Tuatha de Danann had staged a massive storm to prevent them from making land.

"But Amergin's power was great, and he invoked a spell that allowed the Milesians to survive the storm, calling on the spirit of Ireland to provide them safe passage. Though he succeeded, it was not without lives lost. Not the least of whom was Amergin's wife, Scéne, who is immortalized where she fell in the estuary at Inber.

"And so, the kings were slain in single combat, and Amergin divided the land between his brothers, creating what is now Ireland. But while Amergin was victorious, he had suffered perhaps the greatest loss of all, as Scéne was, and still is, the love of his life," he finished somberly.

I experienced the pain and loss keenly, as I supposed was intended. To lose something you love so dearly, to lose the future you could have had, was a pain few understood. Never would my parents see me married, nor would they hold my yet unborn children. I wouldn't get the chance to hear my mother's wisdom when I was with child or listen to the stories of my own childhood as I experienced my children growing up with my mother watching on.

My father wouldn't tell tales as long and windy as a winter's night to my husband. Nor would he teach my babes the same life lessons as he did me.

Unbidden, tears formed in my eyes. I desperately tried blinking them away, but the lump in my throat only grew as I thought of Amergin and his wife.

Never to hold her or kiss her again. He would never have babes who favored her or him, never get to see the glow on her face as she grew swollen with their children or witness the joy as she held them.

Joseph watched in silent observation as those thoughts and emotions shone on my face. He didn't judge or even empathize. All that was in his countenance was resoluteness, sheer will, and determination.

"Surely you can understand why he wouldn't feel inclined to interfere himself, and further, why your account would be motivation enough to prevent more atrocities."

I nodded because that was it—we needed to act so more catastrophes could be avoided. So fewer orphans were created, or widows and widowers. There was no alternative.

"When do we leave?" I finally asked, once I could speak past the emotions still thundering through me.

"Day after tomorrow, or perhaps today, given the hour. We will pack in the morning and hopefully rest well before we depart."

"We?"

"Yes—me, you, and Whalen."

"Who will stay here?"

"Oisin, Michael, and Donal."

"But Oisin is hardly in a position to defend himself, let alone the whole clan," I said, suddenly struck with the possibility that Oisin was arguably better suited than even Whalen now. If only I knew more about shifters.

"He's plenty strong enough, and my men are particularly well suited for the task."

"What about Sloane?" I asked, hoping to keep one of the wolves here if I could.

"She has a different journey for the task before us."

"Which is?"

"Something Whalen can discuss with you rather than me."

"Okay, then," I said. I still had questions, but I was willing to drop it as I tried to yawn as quietly as I could. I wasn't successful.

"Sleep now, as long as you can, since we won't be getting the luxury on the road."

"We won't?" I asked a little sadly, as I'd finally gotten my bed back. I wasn't thrilled to leave it so soon.

"No, *mo bhanríon*, we won't."

"Don't call me 'queen,'" I said, suddenly panicky. Even the word sent a shiver up my spine.

"You would do well to get used to the idea, at least," he said with a twinkle in his eye.

I groaned audibly, and his laughter filled the

quiet room, so warm and inviting that I wanted to curl into it.

The thought alarmed me. Either I was too lonely, or these men were too tempting.

Checking Joseph out for a moment, I took note of his dark complexion and molten eyes, and I concluded it was the men here, not me. His luscious lips quirked upward as I kept looking. Embarrassed, I looked away quickly, but he'd already seen.

There was something deeply wrong with me. I was glad they found it entertaining, at least.

"Get some sleep," he said again, breaking the tension, and I could have kissed him for that alone.

"Final question," I hedged. He had been forthcoming to this point, so why stop now?

"Yes?" he said as he quirked one eyebrow up.

"When did you and Whalen become fast friends?"

"Ah, I was waiting for that one. In the aftermath of the dragon, he approached me that night to *discuss* things. We knew who or what the other was, and we had to come to terms. And during our conversation, it became apparent that we were two forces with the same goal: to crush the opposition. We chose to work together rather than separately, and we formed the plan we have laid before you this evening. Though, that was not necessarily part of the plan," he said with a grin to remind me of my mouth fused to Whalen's not so long ago.

"Good night," I whispered, blushing, rolling over to enjoy the softness of my bed for as long as possible while also hiding my face. "Thank you, Joseph."

"Good night, *mo bhanríon*."

I rolled my eyes even as the knot formed again in my belly. Doubly so given the voyage we were set to embark on.

## CHAPTER
# SEVEN

A WARM HAND NUDGED MY SHOULDER, AND THE SMELL OF coffee made me moan in delight.

"You enjoy being woken up this way, do you? I have another way in mind when you're so inclined," Whalen said, voice getting lower with the insinuation.

"Coffee will do fine, thank you," I said, even as other parts of me woke right up at his words.

He was maddening with his swagger and self-assuredness. Cockiness was normally something I hated in a man, yet his confidence was a second skin. It suited him so well, and truth be told, he had earned the right to it too. Which only made it more frustrating.

"Coffee might do, but my plan will exceed your expectations, if I do say so myself."

"You might be the only one saying it," I said, taking the coffee from him as I sat up.

Wiping the sleep from my face, I looked around for Joseph. He was gone, as were his bed things. *Damn, not even a buffer here.*

"It's late, darling. You're going to sleep the day away if I let you."

I groaned back. Why did he have to keep talking? He was too chipper for me at the moment.

"In all seriousness, it is late. I expect you to be packed before supper."

"Pack what?" I asked, my voice hoarse from disuse.

"Light. The necessities."

"How light?"

"As air. You'll be carrying it all in a pack, so whatever doesn't fit is out."

"But I don't know where to start." I didn't. I'd never traveled long distances before. What would be the most important things to bring?

He turned then and went for the closet across from my bed. I felt a moment of alarm, but I was sluggish without caffeine to kick-start my brain.

"Mmm," he said, pulling out a lacy chemise

intended only for the most formal parties my parents would host. "I think we will most definitely be requiring this."

He held the garment by two fingers in front of him, as if trying to see me in it in his mind's eye. I burned with the indecency of the proposal, though my nether regions thoroughly agreed with his sentiment.

"We most certainly will not," I said, throwing back the covers to join him in the closet before he ransacked all my lacy things.

I drank deeply from my mug before putting it down, letting the heat sear my throat in the most delicious way. A hum sprang out of me at the feeling before I turned my fury toward Whalen.

Gods be damned, but he had bedroom eyes when I turned to face him fully. My retort flew off in the wind.

"Why don't you have another sip first, and then we can pack," he said, and my heart picked up tempo.

He said the words like an innuendo. I obliged him more for the courage the hot liquid would give me than to give in to his commands.

But the pure ecstasy of it got me again, and I savored each sip.

"Tell me we'll have coffee on the road," I nearly begged.

"If it would make you happy, then of course. I wouldn't take that from you."

He seemed so intent, I had to glance away and place my coffee down again to avoid his eyes.

"Then let's get to it," I said, indicating the closet beyond him. He was still giving me the same stare, so I asked, "What?"

I was a little sharper than I meant to be, but I still hadn't gotten the caffeine into my veins yet. It was the one time of day when people should talk to me the least, and here he was, demanding I interact.

"You with your spine of steel," he said with a shake of his head.

"What do you mean?"

He considered how to respond for a beat or two.

"You plow through like the best soldiers I've known. One obstacle after the next, you face it head-on, shoulders squared, and you keep going until the job is done or the next one crops up. That steel was hard-won, I know, but it impresses me all the same."

He said it so sincerely, I was a little uncomfortable at the praise, at the acknowledgment. So I did what I did best and deflected instead of caving to the emotions his words evoked in me.

"You might have the wrong of it. If my spine wasn't steel before, it was at least oak or iron," I said, making a joke of my stubborn streak.

"I don't doubt it, sweetheart, but you undeniably muscle through whatever is thrown at you, and I'm proud of you for it."

Heavens, what was I supposed to do with this man? I was simultaneously on the verge of tears and ready to throw myself into his arms.

"How difficult will this journey be?" I asked to change the subject.

He caught my evasion, if the crinkle in his eyes was any indication, but he let it drop. Turning, he placed my chemise back where it belonged.

"Difficult and then some."

"Is it necessary?" I asked, hoping we could stay where we were comfortable and safe.

"If only I knew, love. It's a gamble to be sure, but it's a bet I'm willing to take. Are you?"

I thought again of my parents. Of the story Joseph told me about Amergin. How many more would lose their lives in this pursuit? Or better yet, how many would if we didn't?

Then a thought crossed my mind.

"What if we lose?"

"What if we don't?"

I gave him a look that told him how much I liked his answer. To my surprise, he gripped my biceps, leaning closer as he did so.

"If you've learned anything yet, sweetheart, it's that nothing is guaranteed. We don't know what will happen in the next minute, much less the next year. But we've got to give it our all, don't we? Or else what's the point?"

My eyes displayed exactly how much I liked *that* answer, and he laughed—a warm belly laugh that had me smiling as well. But the reality of the statement also had me sighing, and I looked away to prevent him from seeing the dread on my face. What was the point?

I clearly didn't hide my emotions well enough, because he reached for my chin, gently coaxing me to look at him again. His touch was light but firm, and I nearly purred in delight at the feel of his warm skin on mine, the sensation of his rough calluses, and the strength even in a simple touch.

"We'll find the reason," he said simply, but I understood the way he meant it.

Find a reason for the pain and the hurt. A reason to keep going despite it, or perhaps in spite of it.

I smiled, a tight-lipped one that conveyed my gratitude but also my doubt.

He reached out with his other hand then, dropping my chin in favor of my shoulders, and I was so
shocked when he pulled me in for a hug that I stum-
bled awkwardly toward him. Gods, but what a hug.

His arms were the greatest of delicacies, so
warm and strong. I savored the moment as if it were
my last meal as I leaned in to return the gesture.
When my hands met with the breadth of his shoulders, I had to bite my lip for fear of biting him. The
urge to sink my teeth into him and claim him was
akin to needing oxygen.

I inhaled deeply, not even caring to hide my
ecstasy at his offering, and I was rewarded with the
woodsy scent that clung to him, the scent of fresh
mountain air. And he was warm, so comfortably
warm, it made goose bumps dance across my skin,
though I hadn't realized I was cold.

Afraid I would overstay my welcome, I forced
myself to relinquish my hold on him enough that he
could end the hug if he desired to. To my delight, he
didn't. Instead, he squeezed tighter, inhaling my
scent as deeply as I had his before placing a hand on
the back of my head and kissing its crown.

Then I truly melted.

My insides turned to liquid as joy erupted in my
belly. A feeling I couldn't quite identify simmered

beneath the joy, something archaic and wild. Tears sprang into my eyes, and I forbid them from fully forming, but they weren't all sad, and that was the problem. They were hopeful tears, and I banished the hope from existence.

There could be no dreaming of tomorrow, I told myself, only the enjoyment of now.

I released a breath I didn't know I needed to, and a weight lifted off my shoulders. All the heaviness I'd been carrying was whisked away in one exhale.

Then he let go. With another squeeze of my shoulders, he pushed back on them until he could look at me once again.

"Thank you," I whispered, feeling both embarrassed and vulnerable—a feeling I didn't appreciate, not one bit.

"Anytime," he said back as he tugged on my hair gently before letting go.

I asked the question that continued to plague me. "Why?" What did it matter to him if I was happy or sad?

"One of life's great mysteries, I suppose," he said teasingly.

He didn't answer my question, but the evasion was clear enough. Either he didn't have an answer or he wasn't ready to divulge it at the moment, so I let it drop with a roll of my eyes.

Part of me was disappointed that it wasn't more than a hug, but I supposed it may have taken some of the meaning out of it had it gone further. I still felt guilty for wanting it, too, knowing Oisin was maybe even in the house now, since Whalen apparently knew all about him.

Perhaps that was why he was respecting my space now. I wondered why, when last night he hadn't. He didn't comment on it, though, only looked around, searching for something.

"You wouldn't have a knapsack or something, would you?" he asked at last.

I did, in fact. Being outdoorsy, my father indulged me with different gear for when we went on adventures ourselves, sometimes fishing or hunting but most often foraging. I headed to the trunk at the foot of my bed, opened it, and held up the bag.

The chest was sturdy and olive green, made of heavy material designed to weather the elements. It was perfect for what was to come next.

"Aye, now what have you to put in it? Do you have trousers and shoes instead of...?" he said, waving at my body to indicate the nightgown I wore.

My cheeks heated then in earnest. I'd all but forgotten the thing, though I didn't know how. Thinking about the embrace again, I realized chances were that he hadn't kissed me because of the implications it would entail with me being barely dressed. A steady throb beat beneath the sheer fabric, and his flaring nostrils told me I hadn't a chance in hell at hiding my feelings. I was seconds away from throwing myself at him when he spoke again.

"Do you?"

"Do I?" I asked, perplexed. I'd lost my mind, it seemed, at the idea of being nearly naked in a bedroom with him.

He didn't hide the grin that split his face. It was a confident one and oh so sexy.

"Have anything else to wear?"

"Oh!" I all but exclaimed, busying myself digging for my clothes to hide the crimson over-taking my face.

Damn my Irish skin.

I quickly pulled out the different outerwear I owned, focusing on the task to bring myself back to normal. I grabbed the heavier items and threw them on the bed, where he inspected them and sorted them. When I finished, he had two neat piles of folded clothes, and he looked impressed.

"You've done more than a few things with your father, then?"

I thought back to the busy man I'd known. I'd always thought him too preoccupied to spend much time with me, and I supposed he was. But a portion of the time was spent in teaching me all he knew. In some ways, his lecturing me was his way of bonding with me.

"It seems so," I said at last, and he nodded.

"This is fine," he said, indicating one pile. "Feel free to comb through it. Do you have boots somewhere?"

"Check beneath the bed," I said, moving to look through his choices.

All the woolen socks were in the pile to take, but only two pairs of pants and three heavy sweaters were in there with them. I grabbed a few of the lighter things and added them.

When he returned, boots in hand, he saw my choices and inspected them.

"They'll do, but you don't want your pack to be too heavy," he said.

"The sweaters aren't fitted to my body. I usually

wear the shirts and stockings beneath both, so it holds my body heat better."

"Right, then," he said, and the smirk made me feel proud, as if he was impressed with my preparedness. A silly thing, but I still glowed under his approval.

"Then toiletries and whatnot. If you're keen on bathing, I would take one before we leave, as you're not going to find one on the road. Pack the bag as light as you can and wear the boots—tomorrow, that is. And eat. Eat 'til you're bursting at the seams. Evelyn is packing as much as she can without it being too much to carry, but there's still no saying how easily we'll be able to resupply in the dead of winter."

I nodded, unsure of what to say to keep my nerves under wraps. It hadn't been too daunting at first, but now the reality was sinking in.

"I'll be giving out my final orders to the men. We leave at first light tomorrow."

"Okay, thank you." I nearly choked on the words, the anxiety hitting me like a ton of stones and making my throat dry. Tension filled the air as seconds ticked by before he spoke again.

"Oisin is downstairs if you want to see him before we leave as well," he spoke at last, his eyes boring into mine. As if in breaking contact, he'd lose whatever he was holding on to.

"Oh, thanks." I wanted to say more, but what, I had no idea. Maybe that I could hardly remember who Oisin was when I looked at Whalen. Or that no one made my blood heat with a look like Whalen could. How could I face Oisin now that I knew these things?

"I'll leave you to it, then," he declared and gently closed the door behind him before I could respond, which was all for the better because my brain had left with him.

*Oisin.* His name beat through me for different reasons than it used to. Before it had been the steady beat of my heart, keeping me moving forward. I didn't know when it began to fill me with dread, but it did all the same.

Pushing that reality to the back of my mind, I busied myself with putting my clothes away. Deciding to bathe now, and perhaps again later, I drew the water next. I'd no sooner sunk into the water when I realized it didn't hold the key to my problems within it. I tried to focus on envisioning the water siphoning out my torment, but it increasingly mimicked a weight trying to drown me.

I realized I'd chosen to bathe to avoid the

meeting with Oisin. But I didn't see any way to prepare for it. Worrying about the feelings I may have toward him and the feelings I'd developed toward Whalen did no good. I had to face it.

While I dressed slowly, a calm washed over me. Not much to do about it, so I may as well accept it. If my fate was to marry Oisin and not be in love with him, then that was the duty I owed my people, and I would do it to the best of my ability. But not before preventing further harm from befalling our clan.

So, without further ado, I decided to go for it and made my way downstairs. It wasn't long before voices drifted up from the kitchen, Evelyn's and Oisin's and a few I didn't recognize.

They heard me before I entered, and conversation politely died out as I walked in. It was almost worse that way.

"Emer" was all Oisin said, and I was glad to see his pallor improved.

"Oisin. Feeling better, I hope?" I asked, feeling more awkward than I thought possible.

"Yes, thank you."

"Well, now, boys, let's make haste. I need help loading the saddlebags," Evelyn said to Michael and Donal, whose voices I now realized were the ones I hadn't recognized.

"Miss," the pair said in unison, nodding at me.

I watched them leave, puzzling over them. I'd need to learn more about the men surrounding Oisin. Though could I even call them men when they were something else entirely?

Was Michael still a man? Or was that part of why it was hard for me to recognize him that time in the barn? If he wasn't, I could only hope it was a choice he'd made and not had forced upon him somehow.

That was when I looked at Oisin, uncertainty coiling in my belly. He was no longer an ordinary man but harsher and cooler. Joseph's habits aside, the Abhartach were hunters, and I was outmatched.

"How are you?" he asked simply, a tentative thing.

I thought of the tumult of emotions roaring inside me. Of the mess that had befallen my home and my family. But I buried all those things.

"I'm fine, thank you. How are you?" I asked, hedging, trying to determine whether he was content with his lot in life.

He smiled, sensing the words I didn't say.

"I'm all right, Emer, really, but how are you?" he asked again, taking a step closer.

His dark eyes and hair were the same hues I'd

known forever, as were the thin bridge of his nose and fair skin. But the delicateness I had always associated him with had been replaced with something sharper, something harder. I didn't balk when he stepped closer, and when he reached out to brush the corner of my new bangs, a little of the wall I had erected between us crumbled.

This was Oisin, my betrothed. A friend I had known and played with. And perhaps we were both changed, but we were still undoubtedly the same.

That realization had me reeling and centered me at the same time. And so I answered him honestly.

"Some days are better than others, but I'm getting through."

And I was. It wasn't a straight line but a jagged one full of boulders and dead ends. I thought of all Oisin had lost, too, and tried to express my sorrow with my eyes.

"I'm good, Emer, truly. I only worry for you," he said as the hand still idly toying with my bangs went to cup my cheek.

"Don't, please. I'll be fine," I said, because I would. I had to be—no other way but to play the hand I'd been dealt.

He smiled then, finally believing my words.

"Your hair looks good," he said at last, dropping his hand.

I wasn't sure how to feel about it. I was a bit bereft at the loss of his touch, yet I felt as if I shouldn't be. But he was to be my husband, or at least that was what my parents had wished. Perhaps it was only the loss of what had been that had sunk its claws in me, the future I had pictured so many times before now irrevocably changed.

"Thank you," I said, looking at the floor before I thought of something. "Wait, did you know?"

"Know about what? Your heritage? I did. It was a big reason my parents wanted a union between us," he said.

The silence was palpable, stretching between us at his words. Neither of us was quite sure how to broach the subject.

"I hold you to no promises, Emer. But if you so choose, I'm more than happy to oblige," he said, and the smirk on his face was equal parts earnest and amused.

"Don't you think our people would want it that way?"

He ran a hand through his hair, his slender fingers easily combing through the soft locks. He was always graceful, but I noted a difference in his movements. He moved like silk, like water now, so smooth it was as if he hardly moved at all.

"Our people might be opposed to a ruler such as me now," he said, looking at me.

"Do you know how anyone fares?"

"Most of the survivors are at my home. My parents had gone to great lengths to defend it before the battle, and it seems it wasn't in vain."

"How did you end up in my barn, then?"

"Ah, naturally, my father and I were among the warriors. When we broke so easily, we charged forward to reform, and my father didn't make it. I lasted a while longer, but when I was wounded, it was closest to your lands, and Joseph wanted me out of immediate danger more than anything. He has been the go-between since." He paused a moment. "My mother sends well wishes," he said at last.

"Your mother? She's all right?" A stab ricocheted through my belly, but I ignored it. My loss shouldn't affect my happiness for him.

"She is more than all right. Having so many to tend to gives her a purpose again. Now she can stop fussing over me for a while. I was heartbroken to hear of your losses, Emer," he said, and the pain on his face had me hiding mine before I lost my composure.

"And I'm sorry to hear of yours as well. But I am glad to hear your mother fares well. What of the girls?"

It was simpler to call my childhood friends that, as we usually did. Though not close, we all were undeniably enmeshed.

"Making my mother stay quite busy. Cara and Fallon lost their father, but they and their mother are as you would expect."

A blithering mess, no doubt. Not to discount their loss, but I could hardly imagine them any less than hysterical without him.

"Erin and her family are fine," he finished. The unsaid words were that of course they were. If her father fought, he would have done it valiantly without a touch of blood on him to boot.

I nodded, gladness and sadness mingling in an uncomfortable soup of feelings I didn't want to examine further. My clan, the people I cared for—at least there was still someone to fight for.

The intensity in his eyes was a flick of a switch, homing in on the part of him that was so different now. Then there was the feeling again inside, the primal part of me saying that I was the prey. It shouldn't thrill me the way it did, but that was probably because I was hardly a hapless victim.

He noticed the steel in my spine the minute it snapped into place. The shiver of fear was replaced by excitement for controversy. The smile on his face was as serene as ever even as he held my gaze, meeting the challenge.

"Not everyone has the same reaction as you, and the ones who do will prove troublesome. People don't want a ruler they fear. They want one they trust. And I'm no longer someone they trust. I'd prefer to change that, to prove myself to them again, and show that I'm still the same man I was."

"But you're no longer a man," I finished for him.

"Precisely," he said with a sad smile.

"Why did you do it? You did decide, right?"

"I did, but it's a long and winding story. One best saved for your return."

A terrible answer, but I said, "Okay," nonetheless.

"Deciding on our betrothal can wait too. Don't hold your heart for me, but if it still calls for me when this is said and done, I will honor your choice. Happily," he added, grabbing and kissing my hand.

He continued to hold it after his declaration

while I pondered his words. Oisin was a stranger, and yet not, but his words meant a lot to me.

"But what do you want?" I asked, torn.

He considered his response, and I was glad for it. I didn't want him to tell me what he thought I wanted to hear; I wanted the truth.

"Also a story for another day, Emer, one I'm glad to share with you, but not now. However, I don't say the words lightly when I say I would be honored to have you be a part of my life," he said, and it was the best yet worst answer he could give.

But one I could be content with, at least for now.

"All right, then," I said, not knowing what else to say.

"Take care of yourself, please. Walsh and Joseph will protect you, I swear it. But all the same, watch out for yourself."

"I will," I promised. "You do the same."

"I will," he echoed before kissing my cheek.

His touch was featherlight but firm where he was still holding my hand as he leaned down. Goose bumps raced over my skin at the gesture—a feeling I wasn't anticipating.

He seemed amused again when he leaned back, and I groaned internally. Everyone knowing my thoughts and feelings without my say-so was getting old.

"I'll see you soon," he said, heading toward the door.

"Soon," I promised as he left.

When the door shut behind him, I immediately raced to the window to watch his retreat. My mind was fuzzy. Why in the world was I so torn? These men were such a pain. Probably I was sad and lonely, and their kindness was a balm to me.

There was a chance that they were only being nice to me, anyway. Sure, Whalen had kissed me, but that didn't seem to be a rarity, I thought, remembering the women in his bedroom. One could argue that Whalen wasn't even being nice to me but rather that he had ulterior motives.

What if Oisin did too? I was an important figure in our clan, set to be the leader. Perhaps they were both jockeying for my hand—Whalen because he had no claim and Oisin because his claim had been undermined.

There was too much to consider, and it made my head hurt. Besides, I had enough on my plate at the moment without considering the implications of what getting involved with either of them would mean.

Turning my attention away from Oisin's retreating figure, I focused instead on Evelyn, who was instructing the men on what to pack into the saddlebags. Then I noticed how large they were. Beyond large, really. Each was the size of Evelyn's torso, and from the looks of it, they were putting the kitchen sink in them.

I headed out the door to see what was going on just as Whalen came slinking around the corner as if he knew I was making my way outside. Perhaps he did, I realized.

"What kind of horses are we riding, anyway?" I called to him across the lawn.

"Horses?" he asked in return with a wicked grin.

My brain was not catching on to whatever he had meant. I furrowed my brow to show my confusion when he swept his hand backward in a grand motion. Looking beyond him, I saw only trees.

Until one of the trees moved.

Then I realized I was looking at the deep green hue of the one dragon, his head swiveling to me as if sensing my attention. My heart leaped into my throat uncomfortably as my stomach twisted.

"No! Nope, not happening. You can cancel the trip or go without me. There's no way I'm riding a dragon," I said as genuine terror set in at the thought.

The shit-eating grin that split Whalen's face was devastating. All his white teeth, with his canines on full display, shone behind those luscious lips. His twinkling eyes and his square jaw were only more defined by his delight.

If it weren't at my expense, I'd probably be breathless right now. Seeing as it was, instead of his handsome face, I only saw red.

"You're out of your fucking mind," I said, the curse surprising Whalen, which only brought more joy to his eyes.

"Aw, sweetheart, are you afraid of heights?" he asked mockingly as he made his way over to me.

Damn it if my knees didn't grow weak. Butter-flies started flapping away in my stomach for different reasons when he stopped in front of me, that stupid, large, deliciously calloused hand lifting my chin again. I let him, and I put as much ferocity into my eyes as I could muster to let him know I most certainly was not getting on the damn thing.

"Heights for one, yes, but for two—it's a drag-on!" I shouted.

He caressed my cheek with one rough thumb,

and I nearly leaned into it and started purring like a kitten.

"Emer, love, if we travel by horse, we won't be there for weeks. Months, even. It's the fastest way. I won't let anything happen to you," he said, dropping his hand at last, the wicked gleam in his eyes taking on a note of sincerity.

I knew I couldn't ride with Whalen. Just the thought of his body pressed tightly behind mine, his hand on my waist, or my hands on his waist? Oh no, nope—also not happening. I tried to quell the desire quickly reaching a throbbing level and only barely managed it.

"Whalen...," I hedged, the pleading in my voice genuine.

"Sweetheart."

Just the one word, but the implications behind it were obvious. The reason we were doing this, the other families we had to fight for, and the duty I had to my people. He recognized the acquiescence on my face, and I wished he would reward me for it with a kiss. Anything to ease the ache that grew in the absence of his touch.

As if he realized the need, too, he ran a hand over my hair, stopping on my shoulder before standing next to me, facing the dragons. He gently nudged me, guiding me forward toward them.

Then I saw the giants, all in varying forms of height and work. The human—maybe human? Or at least normal-sized—men worked side by side with the giants to tend to the dragons. But my attention couldn't be distracted for long as I looked at the winged mythical creatures.

"Have you ever ridden them before?" I asked, disbelieving.

"How do you think we got here?" he asked, giving me a wink.

I supposed in the fray it'd been difficult to decipher whose men had been atop the dragons that razed the landscape. Though, I did recall them searing men and houses alike. Had Whalen been on one? And if he had, was it my clansmen he had targeted with their flames or the men fighting with the Underworld?

He slowed when we reached the green dragon. The beast regarded us with cool eyes. I expected animosity, but as we stood there, his head bowed our way, halting a few feet from us.

I tried to back away, but Whalen placed a hand at the small of my back, urging me forward. I was so nervous, worrying that the dragon could sense my fear. I wanted to beg Whalen to stop, but the words stuck in my throat. I was too afraid any sudden sounds would startle the monster sniffing at me.

Whalen reached out, and to my surprise, the dragon sniffed delicately at his outstretched palm before nuzzling his enormous snout into it. The action was such a domesticated thing to do that I looked at Whalen, who smiled at me. Leaving one hand on my back, he grabbed one of mine and guided it toward the dragon, whose teeth gleamed yellow beneath the nostrils sniffing toward me.

I tried to pull back, but Whalen kept me firmly in his grip until at last I sensed the heat from the dragon's breath on my palm. And it was *hot*.

That alone was jarring, and as he inhaled deeply, I realized the heat wasn't only from his breath but from the animal itself, radiating like hot coals. How was I supposed to ride something so scalding hot?

He exhaled, and I tried not to wince, my cold hands reacting strongly to the heat. But with that exhale, he pressed his snout into my palm, and I couldn't help but marvel.

His skin was rough, reminiscent of bark, and so incredibly hot. It wasn't enough to burn but was shocking enough, like touching a teapot. The forest green of his skin continued in his gaze as he looked into mine with an intelligence far more ancient than I could describe. Something primal in me stirred as I looked into their depths, feeling the weight of their weariness in my soul.

"Naturally, they are best after they're fed, but they aren't too different from horses. Each one has their own personality and preferences. I call this one Saoi. The white one over there is Neart."

When Whalen spoke, I was so entranced, I didn't hear him at first.

"Wise one?" I whispered a few beats later.

"Fits him, don't you think?"

"It does," I agreed.

With Whalen's hand still covering mine, I explored Saoi's snout as much as he would let me. It seemed he was as curious about me as I was about him, because he ventured closer, sniffing at my belly, my hair. The remnants of fear fled as he snuggled against my cheek.

"I thought the two of you would get along famously," Whalen said in my ear as he moved to stand behind me, resting his hands gently on my waist to keep me from falling over at Saoi's gentle exploration.

Though he was being careful, he was still a big thing, moving me around as he continued to sniff at me. Instinctively, or maybe purposely, I leaned farther into Whalen and felt his hands tighten on my hips.

Thoughts of the dragon in my face drifted away as the feel of the White Wolf behind me replaced them. Gods, he was big, his hands engulfing my hips, his body towering over mine. Heat coursed through me, and I bit my lip as fantasies of his hands elsewhere on my body took over.

He agreed with the direction of my thoughts, if the length of him against my back was any indication. His own hips sat near the middle of my back, him being much taller than me. The firmness he pressed against me begged for me as much as I craved to explore it.

I wasn't sure when Saoi moved away from us, as my eyes had closed of their own volition. But eventually, I noticed the absence, breaking the trance I had fallen into.

Embarrassed and frazzled, I removed Whalen's hands from my hips and took a step away from him. Glancing around before turning to face him, I didn't see any of his men, thank goodness. I would have died on the spot if anyone were a witness to what had just occurred between us.

"Emer," he gasped, his voice low and rough.

But I couldn't. Though Oisin had released me from any promises, I couldn't shake the duty I still felt, the promise I'd made to him and my parents. And though I knew Whalen was not directly responsible for what happened to my parents, there were still more stories to contend with, more I didn't know about him.

I felt the loss of his touch keenly, but I shook my head. Whalen stopped reaching for me, the light in his eyes dying out in a rush. Silence stretched taut between us, neither knowing what to say nor having the breath to say it.

"We leave at first light," he said then and stalked away from me.

"Whalen," I called after him, my voice a feeble thing.

I didn't even know what I meant to say. All that mattered was keeping him near me.

He didn't seem to agree, as his long strides carried him away from me quickly, his shoulders hunched and his fists clenched.

Depression crashed through me, rearing its ugly head. The loneliness, the sadness, and the lost feeling overpowered me, threatening to consume me.

Why did I push him away?

Sinking to my knees, I sat on the cold ground, snowmelt seeping through my clothes, but I barely noticed it. I knew Oisin held me to no promises, but he said he'd happily fulfill them. Didn't I want to be with Oisin?

Thoughts of his kindness, of his gentleness crossed my mind, and I thought of him fondly. But he didn't set me on fire the way Whalen did.

Oisin was safe and comfortable, though. Whalen dripped danger; he oozed excitement. Which made him popular with more women than solely myself, I remembered bitterly.

I was tired—bone tired, soul tired, the kind of tired sleep and rest could no longer fix. The kind that dulled the senses, that wrapped me in a blanket of ice I hoped would never thaw. Perhaps that was it. Maybe Whalen thawed the frozen wasteland I had built for myself in a way that was threatening to my self-preservation.

If I let him in and he let me down, was it something I could survive? I wasn't so sure anymore.

A part of me had died right along with my parents and the clansmen we'd lost. It seemed vital to my survival to not let more people in. The ones I had, I could keep; I didn't see any other choice. But to open my heart to more people was like walking on thin ice. One wrong step and I'd drown.

*Damn it.*

Either way, it seemed a waste. To be with Whalen for how long? Until I got back and tried to be with Oisin? Could Whalen lead my people? Would he even want to?

Did *I* even want to?

What a mess.

I wanted to bury myself in the cold earth beneath me right alongside everyone I mourned. How could I save more people if I couldn't even save myself?

Hot breath steamed in my ear as Saoi investigated. The fear that bubbled up at first was gone completely, mellowing into a gentle inquisitiveness. I marveled at his tranquility as I ran a hand under his snout.

"Oh, wise one, can you help me find the answers I seek?" I asked jokingly.

While I wondered at how tame he was, I also examined him more closely. The shimmering skin that was so rough to the touch and looked more like a snake's rather than a fish's. Horns sprouted above his nose, his eyes, and partially down his neck.

The ones closest to me were bony, while the

ones on his neck were scaly. His wings were tucked in close but hung loose, which allowed me to examine their fragility from here. Though tougher than they looked, I was sure, they still seemed more like glass wings than something that would carry a beast as big as him through the skies.

Those weblike wings moved closer suddenly, and I realized how near I was to him. His chain still had a lot of give to spare as he moseyed his way to sit beside me. His heat spread through me, a blazing inferno, and I shivered. I hadn't realized how cold I had grown.

Perhaps he did.

Settling himself around me, he wrapped his long tail around my seated figure and laid his head down quite similarly to a dog with his hand outstretched in front of him. Or claws?

I took the first deep breath in what felt like ages, my breath whooshing out in one gust with what was left of my flagging strength. Leaning back against Saoi, I sat and watched the clouds float by in amicable silence.

I DIDN'T KNOW HOW LONG I SAT THERE, BUT LONG enough that the day bled away into evening. A part of me felt guilty for the listlessness, and yet I couldn't have summoned any activity if I tried. And the gods knew I didn't try.

I patted Saoi in thanks and goodbye, and he chuffed a salutation back. *Until tomorrow*, we seemed to say.

Tomorrow was why I didn't mind the lazy afternoon today. I would more than make up for my lethargy. Something deep inside me was soothed by my time with Saoi, as if he truly were a wise one, an ancient soul. Though I supposed he was.

A certain magic existed in those moments with creatures who allowed you to be. With no clocks to be wound and no agenda. And the woods.

If I hadn't said it out loud yet, a part of me was thrilled to be back in the woods. Even the patch of green that I lay in with the dragon let me soak up a heady combination of peace and vitality. To allow me to reenergize and relax at the same time. There simply was no other elixir like it.

But the deep woods was where my heart soared, what it ached for. I didn't know that I realized how much I'd missed the rich scent of dirt and pine, the bitter wind on my cheeks, the sunlight dappling through the canopy, dancing with the little elves who were surely underfoot, tucked away in hollows and rabbit holes.

The memories of being out with my father foraging for different herbs or patiently awaiting a deer brought tears to my eyes. Some were for my father, who I missed dearly. But mostly it was the yearning for the trees, the pining after the adventure, the ecstasy of wanderlust.

Suddenly tomorrow couldn't come soon enough.

I bounded through the house to find Evelyn ready to serve dinner. Oisin awaited me, as did Joseph and his men. Even Sloane was there, standing stoic at the door to the hallway. But no Whalen.

I swallowed back the disappointment and greeted everyone cheerfully. But even after the joyful dinner, I laid my head down in bed and had to squash the unhappiness coursing through me.

# CHAPTER
# EIGHT

Morning dawned slowly, Joseph waking me before the first tendrils of light graced the sky. He left me to dress in the darkness, the purple sky as blank and starless as I was.

Nerves didn't rankle me, nor did the brief excitement I had found yesterday return. Only a yawning emptiness. I wished for the sky to swallow me in its vastness, but it only stared back at me with indifference.

Joseph handed me a coffee when I made my way downstairs. Evelyn was up, bustling her way through the kitchen to prepare us a hearty breakfast that would last us the day. We wouldn't break until nightfall, making a camp in the twilight. We would eat only what we had packed.

Evelyn had put smoked venison and salmon, which I wasn't even aware we had, into the packs we'd be carrying. She said Sloane had come with rows of fish strung together on a rope like a morbid necklace when I was watching the clouds drift by yesterday.

"Be careful now, dear, and come back to me. You promise me," Evelyn said, hugging me tightly to her.

"I promise. Take care of yourself, too, please?"

She nodded, her eyes shining behind her smile.

"You knew?" I asked, unsure when or if I would get the chance to next.

"Better yet, I knew first," she said as she winked at me.

"What do you mean?"

"You were sharp even as a babe, always observing the world around you. Your father had to stay quiet, and I wasn't hired only for my exceptional culinary skills. I have secrets of my own, a story for another day, but as you grew, it became more obvious. The way you have a *knowing* that others don't. And the way you always knew how to weave situations in your favor.

"I brought it to your father's attention. Your mother seemed like she was about to figure it out, but it was important that he knew so he could start to train you. To help you understand, and to conceal your inclinations better. Though I fear you had a way of getting the better of your father despite his best efforts. A young woman as beautiful as you, as powerful as you, dating! Choosing her own husband. That can only be explained by your powers, darling, because your father was not a man to be trifled with.

"Maybe it was his love for his only daughter. But the way you seemed to speak to the world around you, and it to talk back, that was something only someone truly gifted could master, as you have always done.

"That was another reason I called you 'Sarah.' For the way you were able to command situations and act as if it were only natural. Perhaps it was, but nonetheless, it was a wonderful performance."

An actress, I mused. I'd never felt as if I were acting anything out, only reacting to life as it happened. My ability to navigate through situations was something I had only attributed to my father's training. In a way, maybe those were one and the same, both natural and taught.

"I'm not sure I understand," I said at last.

"You will, as I did, and your father had as well.

All in due time, love," she said with a kiss on my cheek before shooing me on my way.

And with that, I was off into the indigo sky. The cold bit at my face, the only exposed part of me, but I finally felt like I could breathe.

"Emer!" Evelyn called from the doorway.

I turned to look, sure I forgot something.

"You can have pity-party days but not a pity-party life," she said before closing the door and peeking through the curtain to wave.

I rolled my eyes, but I smiled, which was the desired effect. She said it often. You could have down days, but you couldn't live your life feeling bad for yourself. What a shame to waste the gift you were given, she would say, the gift of life, when so many were less fortunate.

The words rang truer than ever.

I waved back, a little more pep in my step. It wasn't perfect, but I had more than others. I owed it to my parents, who died for me, to fight for the gift they had given me. To claw my way back to the land of the living instead of crawling into an early grave.

Gods, but quitting was much easier.

Shaking it off, I followed Joseph at a quicker pace, eager to see Saoi. How was that for living? I had the chance to ride a dragon, something I could say in truth no other human I knew, alive or dead, had the privilege to do.

But I did.

And I was ready for it.

Saoi met me at the edge of his enclosure in the woods. He seemed excited at the prospect of spreading his wings again. How he knew that was what we were about to do, I couldn't say, but he was all but wagging his massive tail in his haste.

A saddle was brought out, and Joseph went through the motions, instructing me along the way. I'd never known there were saddles made for dragons, but this one certainly wasn't made for a horse.

Chills ran through me a moment before his voice rumbled in the quiet.

"Ready?" was all Whalen said, a concession in its own.

"Yeah," I said, breathless, my traitorous eyes meeting his. I knew the need shining in them was obvious.

I tried to tamp it down, but it was quickly snuffed out by his dismissal. He looked at Joseph, who nodded.

"Let's go, then," he said, walking away without a second thought.

Joseph climbed into the saddle with grace, his

lithe body whispering against the leather straps and buckles. When he offered a hand down to me, I took it, clambering up with significantly less fluidity than he did.

Settling myself in front of Joseph as he instructed, I gripped the pommel as he reached his arms out around me to take the reins. His warmth seeped through the layers of clothing, and I was grateful we were doubled up because I had no clue how to manage this thing.

"You've done this before?" I craned my neck to ask him.

"Many times, Your Highness," he said in my ear. "Now hold on."

He kicked his heels into Saoi's sides, and the beast lumbered forward, beginning a slow walk that graduated to a run. When he unfurled his wings, panic slammed into me, and my mouth went drier than a desert, my heart beating like the wings of a hummingbird.

Joseph held on to my waist with one strong arm, his other hand still holding the reins. Truthfully, the dragon didn't need his guidance at the moment, as his wings beat in steady thunderous booms and we were lifting off the ground.

I had to close my eyes tight as the ground was

whisked away from me. I was white-knuckling the pommel, and I squeezed the saddle with every ounce of strength as Saoi took us skyward.

To the beast's credit, the transition was smooth. One moment I felt every step vibrate through me, and the next I was floating in the sea. Except we were in the sky.

The sun chose that moment to peek over the horizon, as if to mark the journey with its presence. Sunshine and new days, it promised—a new beginning.

Eventually, I braved more than a squint, and I swallowed terror at the sight of the ground thousands of feet below us, though I still squeaked. I already knew that I was afraid of heights, though I had also never been this high before. Now I could *confidently* say that I was most assuredly afraid of heights.

"Breathe, Emer. He'll sense your unease. You trust him, don't you?"

I nodded; I did trust Saoi. What I didn't trust was the world. It had a wicked sense of humor.

But I did as he said and gulped air into my lungs. I had wrapped a scarf more tightly than usual around my face and wore a hat low on my brow to block the wind, so air came hot and humid through the layers, but it did come, all the same.

I relaxed enough that Joseph released his death grip on my stomach and took an easier one holding the reins close to me. Cradled in his arms, I was comforted, but the pang of regret at them not being Whalen's arms still crept into my consciousness.

Looking around, I didn't even see Whalen anywhere.

Joseph caught my worried glance and shouted in my ear again.

"There," he said, pointing out a speck far to the right.

He was hard to make out, but against the white snow in the horizon, there was a black figure that moved along with us. It wasn't until the trees overtook the landscape a moment later that I realized he had ridden the white dragon, his pale scales a perfect camouflage for the snowcapped mountains we headed toward.

It made sense—like calls to like. The two of them could be ghosts in these woods, blending in perfectly. The same with us and Saoi, I realized a moment later. Perhaps that was why Whalen had chosen the way he did. If he did choose.

With each passing minute, I settled in further to

the rhythm of the wingbeats and the reassurance of Joseph behind me. He was remarkably comfortable.

His arms were still wrapped around me, holding firmly, and he provided enough resistance that I could sink backward against him a bit and ease the strain on my back. I asked him several times if he needed me to lean forward, but he insisted that being a vampire had advantages I should exploit.

Talking was difficult, though, so questioning him about said advantages would have to wait. Frankly, I wasn't sure I wanted to know all about them anyway. It made the reality of the Abhartach too concerning. I wasn't sure I wanted to know all their secrets, but there was a distinct benefit if I could learn them.

That was something for later, though. Instead, I enjoyed the rolling hills of the landscape, the trees, and the glens. In the distance, towns grew, and houses on the outskirts became visible, increasing in quantity and relation to one another before the densely populated areas became visible.

Smoke curled lazily from chimneys, reminding me how cold I was. I no longer shivered, though; it was mostly a solid numbness that existed throughout my body.

As we neared the towns, we got closer to the

tree line so we could blend in better. But getting closer allowed me to see the images with more clarity.

What I thought was smoke from cookfires and hearths was in reality much grimmer. Husks remained where houses once stood, the supporting walls and foundations all that were left of family homes and farms. Scorched earth surrounded not only the remnants but also the fields of wheat and hay meant for animals who lay strewn either slaughtered and burned or were wandering aimlessly, lost without masters.

The solitary farms we passed on the outskirts seemed untouched, but the ones nearing the villages were all in different stages of disarray. My hand reached out to grip Joseph's forearm of its own accord, trying to grasp reality with a touch.

"The queen," he said in my ear, squeezing me in comfort.

"It wasn't only us," I gasped, floundering.

"No, *mo bhanríon.*"

I'd listened to the stories, but seeing was different from believing. The destruction we had thought was left in Whalen's wake didn't end with us, it seemed. I didn't know why I was surprised. It should have been obvious. If my clan had failed to stop the men harassing the countryside, then surely they had continued their onslaught.

Suddenly what we'd set out to do made much more sense. That was if I could believe that I was somehow important in ending this destruction, of course. Perhaps another thing I'd have to see for myself.

White obscured my peripheral vision, and it broke my concentration. Whalen sat astride his dragon, blond hair elaborately braided against the wind, something I hadn't noted before. He looked every bit as fierce as the legends told: broadsword strapped across his back, weapons decorating his belt and his legs, a quiver and arrows hanging from the saddle.

He was breathtaking.

The stern look on his face brooked no argument as he nodded for us to follow, and Joseph shifted the reins to lead us away from the town. We flew low and fast until we reached a deserted loch and found purchase on its shore, the sandy soil our landing strip.

Joseph hopped down first before reaching out a hand to me that I took gratefully, much shakier than anticipated. My legs were jelly, and I had to walk around a little before I got the feeling back in them.

"What's happening?" I asked, though I was grateful for the rest.

"They'll think we did it," Joseph said softly, and I looked at him for an explanation.

Whalen gave it instead.

"We're on dragons, riding over towns burned to hell," he growled, anger and sorrow marking his words.

My stomach dropped. It hadn't occurred to me.

Whalen pulled out a map and set it down on the sand before kneeling in front of it. Joseph went to hunker beside him, the two of them mapping out a different route.

"If we assume every village is like that one, we need to hug the coast instead," he said with a sigh.

"What's wrong with that?" I questioned.

"Our mounts won't blend in as nicely," Joseph said, glancing at the white and green scales glittering in the sunlight.

Both dragons drank deeply from the loch, seemingly unconcerned with us. They were untethered, I noticed, and I glanced at Whalen in alarm, but he was staring at the map still.

"And storms," he said ominously.

"The same storm that batters the coast will reach the mountains as well," Joseph said.

"Aye, but without the cover," Whalen said, finally looking up at him.

A weariness overtook him then, a vulnerable expression transforming his face. I'd never seen him seem so young. It was as if in turning to Joseph for counsel, he suddenly lost himself.

"There's plenty if you know where to look. We'll map it out," Joseph said, leaning closer to the map again.

I left them to it and went to grab a drink. Nibbling at some of the food Evelyn had packed, I waited for them to finish deliberating.

It was easy to forget all my worries here. Though cold, the loch remained unfrozen, and the wind rippled the water into tiny whitecaps. I sat down and leaned against a pine, breathing in the crisp air.

The space was so quiet, the only sounds coming from the whisper of the trees as they creaked and rustled and the loch with its waves gently lapping the shore. Something about it eased the depression that had taken root in my belly, replacing it with hope. The promise of peace settled in my bones, and I was invigorated.

When they came to find me at last, it was with some sadness that I left my spot near the water. But I left with purpose.

WE MADE CAMP NEAR A RIVER THAT LED TO THE OCEAN. We found a clearing tucked away that was big enough for a tent and both dragons, and we tied them up after letting them drink from the river.

Whalen headed out to secure a meal for us all if possible while Joseph and I built a fire and unrolled the bedding. The work was quiet, and I couldn't have been happier. Exhausted from the day's travel, I was ready to curl up and sleep already.

We sat on a pair of rocks, staring at the fire in silence, both lost in thought. Or he was. My brain couldn't focus on much beyond the flickers of light that danced along the logs, the way it occasionally popped and sizzled.

I adored the smell of fire, but now it evoked a

different feeling. For a moment, I imagined limbs instead of logs, the remnants of the townsfolk in my own clan and the ones we passed earlier. Jerking my head away suddenly, I saw yellow eyes staring back, the only thing visible against the backdrop of snow that covered the forest we sheltered in.

We sat locked in silent communication for a moment. I could have sworn the same melancholy plaguing me was reflected in the wolf's calculating eyes. And then they were gone.

The dragons stirred in turn, each huffing with enthusiasm before turning toward the woods. Wet and crunching noises echoed through the silence, and I winced slightly when flames shot from their mouths.

Trotting out of the woods a moment later, the large frame of the wolf became visible as he moved through the clearing in front of us, bloodred interspersing the white. In his jaws was a rabbit, the brown animal flopping around haphazardly in death. He placed dinner at Joseph's feet before heading back into the woods again.

The rabbit still needed cleaning, and Joseph went off to the river to skin and gut it. It hit me a moment later that he might very well be draining the tiny creature of blood while he was at it. Perhaps that was why Whalen had left it whole.

I sat alone for what felt like an hour but was probably only twenty minutes or so. The first to arrive was the wolf again, his fur wet but clean now. He huffed at me before lying near the fire across from me and closing his eyes, though his ears stayed alert.

Uncertainty wended through me, but my face remained passive. If he wasn't in the mood for talking, then neither was I.

Pretending my feelings weren't hurt was easier than stopping the emotions gnawing at my insides. I reminded myself that it was for the better. Oisin was meant to lead with me, and I was sure our people would welcome him with open arms.

I tried telling myself that Whalen wasn't suited for leading, but it was a lie I couldn't sell. I'd seen him with his people and the way they admired him.

But I knew that wasn't why this hurt so much. Somehow, he had whittled his way past my defenses. And as soon as he was within, I kicked him back out.

I'd been cowardly and cruel, and I couldn't forgive myself for my selfishness. I supposed neither could he.

Unless he had no feelings for me. What if it all had been about lust for him and nothing more? And when I shoved him away from me, he saw that I had feelings where he did not, and that was why he was so closed off now, for both our sakes.

My head was spinning right along with my heart when those ears twitched, alerting me to Joseph's approach. I hadn't a clue how he heard anything, because not even ice crunched that I could hear, but Joseph was there in a moment with the rabbit ready for the spit.

The spit I hadn't set up, I realized after a second, too lost in my brain. I scrambled up, grabbed a few large sticks, and quickly carried them back to the fire.

Joseph went to take one out of my hand, and I told him with my eyes he didn't have to, but he grabbed my fingers and made me release it anyway. I felt guilty as it dawned on me that the rabbit was mine alone, but of course Joseph helped me as he had a habit of doing.

I'd hoped that once the hare was cooked, Whalen would join me, but as Joseph quartered what I would eat tonight and what would be saved, Whalen remained motionless. Joseph and I made small talk while I ate, and before long, the time to sleep was upon us.

I made my way to the lone tent and held the door back, seeing if anyone was joining me. Neither of them seemed to pay me any mind.

"Aren't you going to sleep?" I looked at Joseph, unwilling to pay attention to Whalen, who still resembled a stone where he'd settled himself earlier.

"No need," he said with a wink. "We'll keep watch."

"Right. Good night, then," I said, daring a glance toward the wolf, who yet again showed no signs of movement.

Stifling a groan, I closed the tent flap behind me, ignoring the layers I was wearing and crawling beneath the blankets fully clothed. I shivered then, defrosting, though I had forgotten how cold I was. Once the heat settled around me, I fell asleep soundly.

WE WOKE EARLY AND WENT THROUGH THE SAME MOTIONS as the day before, and then again the day after that. That pattern repeated for a number of days, during which Whalen did not speak to me and mostly remained in wolf form.

Joseph and I had fun, though, exploring the woods and foraging for different items. He was pleasant company and a good conversationalist. The discussion never turned toward Whalen, though, both of us feeling anxious as we got closer to our destination.

While we were breaking our fast one morning—or I did, at least—Whalen flew to his paws, suddenly alert. Joseph didn't seem to move at all, but with his speed, he didn't need to, I supposed.

I was about to ask what was going on when a figure emerged from the shadows. He was tall and elegant with dark hair and blue eyes, wearing a cloak the color of the trees. His smile was charming, but the warmth didn't reach his eyes.

"Emer," he said, looking directly at me.

I was about to flounder unattractively or maybe even aggressively demand how he knew me when I realized he was who we were coming to meet. My mind had inadvertently conjured images of a stooped old man, weathered and cranky.

This beguiling man did not match the one in my imagination.

"Amergin," Joseph said politely as Whalen emitted a low growl.

"Abhartach, Púca," he said, addressing them by what they were instead of by name.

I realized he may have known when and where to find us if the stories about Druids could be believed. And if that were the case, he'd possibly planned this meeting for when Whalen was in wolf form, a show of power.

"Amergin," I said by way of greeting. "I hope this means we're close, then."

"Are you so eager to leave such fine company as this?" he sneered, an easy quip that was answered by a growl from Whalen.

"Oh, they're coming with me," I said with authority. "Or are we not welcome here?"

I was not a fan of his demeanor.

"Plucky," he said, giving me a once-over.

"Egotistical," I said, giving him one back.

He laughed then, a deep, rumbling one. I wasn't sure if it was genuine or not, but I was once again mistrusting this quest of ours.

When he was done, he looked at me with contempt. Well, at least we were past the facade.

"Come," he said, and he turned, not waiting for us to follow.

Whalen stalked ahead, pausing only long enough for me to reach him, Joseph bringing up the rear. I didn't know if they thought there was an ambush or some kind of trap, but their hypervigilance was like a weight surrounding me.

We were guided to a heap of rocks leading into the ocean. As we neared it, I noticed that instead of one mass of rock beaten by the ocean, they were all hexagonal columns of varying heights, each identical in diameter.

"Giant's Causeway," I whispered in awe.

I hadn't realized how close we were. If I had known, I would have happy followed just for this sight.

The legend went that Finn McCool, a giant of Fomorian descent, created the causeway to reach Scotland to fight his rival, a Scottish giant named Benandonner. My heart skipped a beat from excitement to see so many of my childhood fantasies come to life.

Amergin threw his first glance back at me, a quizzical look on his face. I narrowed my eyes in annoyance, and he coolly looked forward again, as if he couldn't be bothered with my presence.

I quietly wished Finn McCool could come and step on him. At least squish his ego a bit.

He led us into a crack between columns, the entrance strangely both there and not there. I expected it to be dark and damp inside, the walls closing in on us. Instead, we walked into an open area as big as any living room.

The walls and floor were rock, the walls in the same form as the columns from above. There were sparse furnishings throughout, which made it oddly welcoming. I didn't imagine he had many visitors.

"I thought I would need some furniture for this," he said as if he'd read my thoughts. "No, I don't read minds. I only see glimpses of the future—something I imagine you'll experience for yourself soon enough."

I rolled my eyes and found yellow ones watching me keenly once I was finished. Looking quickly away, I examined the rest of the area as Joseph and Amergin swapped stories. It seemed that though the Druid was standoffish and rude, he had a stake in this war, one he took seriously, if the fervor with which he spoke could be believed.

There were herbs and random items in stacks and piles on different tables around the room. There was a mortar and pestle atop one, varying shells on another, and one wall was dedicated to stones of every size, shape, and color imaginable.

I gravitated toward the wall, resisting the urge to touch them. Two in particular stood out to me, one black as night and the one beside it red with black spots throughout.

A white one caught my eye next, and I looked at the wolf surreptitiously. He watched me still, golden eyes unblinking.

"Emer," Amergin called from the other side of the room.

My name on his lips made me want to cringe. I nearly ordered him to call me *bhanrĩon* as Joseph did, but hearing him call me queen would only annoy me. There was an edge to the way he said my name, a possessiveness he presumed that grated me.

I looked at him lazily, taking my time. If he was going to be presumptuous, then so was I.

He noted the small power play with a raised eyebrow but didn't comment on it. I batted my long lashes at him in mock innocence, and the smirk he gave me then was genuine.

"Druids are the defenders of knowledge, the weavers of fate. It's no small task you accept by doing this."

I looked at him with the most aloof expression I could muster. If he had a point, let him get to it.

"We will see if you're worth your mettle," he said then, dismissing me again.

*I'll show you mettle,* I thought with venom. I didn't know what his deal was, but I was over it already.

A cauldron hung over the fire in an alcove on the wall to my far left. The fire was only embers now, but the room was still warm. I noted no bed, but who knew if another secret room hid beyond one of the columns.

Something wet met my palm, and I nearly squealed in alarm. Whalen's snout nudged me before he came to sit at my feet, and I was so surprised, I had to tell myself to shut my mouth when I found it agape. Reaching out a tentative hand, I stroked the fur along his neck in thanks.

I was surprised by the texture, which was much wirier than I had anticipated, though I didn't know why I'd imagined it would be soft, especially not after so many nights spent watching him sleep outside and hunt game.

Joseph noticed the stance first and began the exit strategy, but Amergin caught wind of it too. He turned to examine our postures, but instead of mockery, ice coated his features.

"Bring her in the mornings, and I will bring her

back to your camp at night. There's no need for us all to be crammed in here every night," he said, dismissing us.

"We will stay with you during the day," Joseph said with finality.

"Don't trust me, old friend? You should know better," he said, and an understanding passed between them that was lost on me.

"Amergin" was all Joseph said as he went for the doorway. It was a warning in one word.

Whalen paced in front of me as Joseph led the way out. It was strange and abrupt, but all I could do was follow.

"See you tomorrow, honey," Amergin said behind me, and I cringed but nodded in acknowledgment.

We made haste back to camp, though I wasn't totally sure why. I knew animosity existed between them, particularly between Whalen and the Druid, but the whole exchange was awkward to say the least.

At camp, the wolf took off. I wished I could say I was surprised, but alas, it was left to Joseph to explain things to me again.

"What was that?" I asked, stirring the embers

until they glowed brightly again before feeding more wood to the fire.

Another love of mine. Fire had a way of speaking to me, the complexity and subtlety combining in an alluring way. It took coaxing, and though it asked for little, it could take so much.

"A pissing match," he said succinctly.

I supposed that was the gist of it.

"But why so much tension? We're all here for the same thing, aren't we?"

"Ah, Amergin has ulterior motives, to be sure. He's harmless to you, though. You have my word."

He seemed serious enough, but I wasn't convinced.

"Then why do the two of you need to escort me daily? And be there for *whatever*," I added, waving a hand around to indicate my complete lack of a clue as to what I was about to do.

He chuckled, the first smile I'd seen from him in quite a while, I realized. Was it me who had been withdrawn or him?

I'd probably have to hazard a guess that I had been the melancholy one, seeing as I may have been moping a smidge since my fight with Whalen—if a fight was what our spat was.

"He harbors some ill will toward Whalen, and

though I know he won't harm you, it's not to say he won't use you to harm Whalen."

I chewed on that for a moment. Excitement stirred in my belly, and I did my best to quell it before it grew wings, but if I had the right of it, Joseph might be saying what I'd been secretly hoping for. That I *could* be used against Whalen.

Not that I was saying I wanted to be, only that I wanted to mean enough to him for it to be possible for me to be used against him.

"Harm him how?" I hedged.

It was the safest way to ask what I was too afraid to. How did Whalen view me?

"*Mo bhanríon,* you hold sway over Whalen. Don't doubt it," he said with a twinkle in his eye.

Ah, but the wings were breaking out of their pupas.

"Sway how, exactly?" I braved.

"That's for him to tell you," he said, nodding to a spot behind me.

I gulped because I already knew who I would see. When I turned to look, however, I was nearly knocked off my perch to see Whalen in human form, shirtless, with ire in his eyes.

Heat coursed through my veins at the sight of him.

Impossibly, he was more handsome with the square set of his jaw and shoulders on full display. That swath of hair I had glimpsed the night I saw him with those women was there, and I could now confirm that tattoos occupied the whole of his chest as well.

Apparently, I had a thing for passionate men. Fine, angry men, but only well-placed and responsible anger.

He snapped the tree limb he'd been holding across his knee before throwing each half into the wood pile and letting out a growl. If I were truly frozen, I would be a puddle right now.

"Fuck!" he spat, his shoulders hunched and fists clenched.

I must have been lost in a haze for a moment, because I was only vaguely aware that Joseph answered. I repeated it in my head a few times until I finally got it.

"He's trying to get under your skin. It seems to me it worked" was what he had replied.

Whalen didn't respond to that. Twitching his neck as if to relieve the tension, he rolled his shoulders back until he was content with his state of aggression. One deep breath and he was more normal. I was strangely sad about it.

"Why must he torture me?" Whalen asked, pacing back and forth across the packed earth.

I wish I had a clue what was going on, but interrupting didn't feel quite right either. If they wanted to tell me, they would. Though if they didn't want me to know, they wouldn't be having this conversation in front of me either.

"It's neither the time nor the place. The thing to be worried about is that our dragons aren't the only ones who have been spotted."

"There are more?" I gasped.

"Yes," Joseph answered again, and I realized Whalen still hadn't spoken a word to me.

"Well, where? And why?"

"That's the question, *mo bhanríon.*"

Whalen still paced, one hand worrying a knife at his belt. I noticed the way he rubbed his thumb over the hilt, and I couldn't help but think of how said hand would feel against my skin. Then I remembered I needed distance and how he had been a jerk to me, and I looked anywhere but at him.

"The queen operates on her own agenda," he mumbled almost to himself. "Did he say what the other dragons looked like?"

Joseph quirked his head funnily but answered with "You know what the *dragon* looks like."

"Caorthannach," he said and punched a tree.

The sound echoed, and the tree shook, though it did not fall.

I knew the legends of Caorthannach, the mother of demons. Said to be immortal, she lay in wait for when she could strike next. But I was failing to put the pieces together.

"The queen will either hold that card over our heads or play it and many will die. She's hoping to usurp Dagda," Joseph said in answer to my quizzical look.

"But he has legions of men. He's fought and won before," I said, disbelief coating my words.

The wars of my childhood were bloody, devastating the world as we knew it. When people thought of war, it was easy to think of it as far off and away, somewhere else. Civil wars were anything but.

During those times, the Druids were targeted for their abilities to weave magic in the wielder's favor. Or they were hunted down and murdered to prevent their ability to do exactly that.

The worst was families of gifted men and women being targeted and used against them. Druids weren't often swayed by wars. Taking sides had little appeal to them, as their side was good for all, and war was the opposite. In their wisdom, they had always been neutral and revered for their stoicism.

My heart sank in my chest.

"My father hid me from them. But they knew he was gifted. We weren't collateral damage in a war we had no place in. We were targeted," I said, reality dawning on me.

Amergin wasn't hidden in a land rumored to be haunted because he was a hermit, fearing others out of neuroses. He was sequestered away, kept safe either by the Great King himself or by the people his vows had sworn to protect.

And I was about to join him.

"Legions of men have not fared well against dragons, my lady," Joseph said softly. "The stakes are much higher than we had anticipated."

"But my father...." I trailed off, no real thought behind it, only the gaping hole he left behind in my soul that seemed to yawn endlessly in the face of my new revelation.

"He was a good and talented man. Well respected and protected. But the queen must have intel. Dagda had a weakness, and she's exploited it to detrimental effect."

A thought crossed my mind, then, since family was used against the Druids.

"Amergin," I said, but it was enough to convey my meaning.

"Lost dearly as well, and has made sure he had nothing left to lose since," Joseph said in answer.

Whalen continued to pace, and the animosity in it was overpowering. I could imagine him as the wolf moving similarly through the little clearing. My battered emotions took another hit as I looked at him with new insight. I'd been right to push him away; it would keep him safe. I hoped he'd walked away because he knew the truth in it, the wisdom.

It didn't make my heart hurt any less. But this reinforced my resolution.

Whalen and Joseph became locked in quiet conversation, but I didn't mind being out of the loop as I considered Amergin's loss and how he had shut himself up in a sepulcher since. Alive and yet not at the same time. Was that to be my fate as well?

I supposed I understood his demeanor if I took that into consideration. Had he been tucked away all these years since the wars? What if he had been squirreled away even before them?

The idea made me sympathize with him, or perhaps empathize. Wait, was I about to be locked up in there with him for decades?

I couldn't interrupt their conversation. They spoke too heatedly, and I still had yet to break the silence with Whalen. And I wasn't going to be the one to do it.

Instead, I busied myself gathering more firewood around the little clearing. Nothing to worry about in these woods. The ghost of Finn McCool scared people away, and perhaps they were onto something, because animals shied away from the area too. Whenever Whalen hunted, he had to go miles away and oftentimes for the entirety of the day to acquire more meat for the dragons.

I, on the other hand, subsisted on what Evelyn had packed and whatever we foraged for, which in winter wasn't much, but I didn't need a ton to survive on.

Apparently, vampires did not require much to sustain them, as Joseph would go as long as I or longer between true meals. The longer he went between feedings, the more secluded he would become, sometimes not talking to me for days. I didn't entirely mind. The quiet was renewing.

There was more to the woods than only my affinity for them. They were a magical place, and many creatures and gifted people would retreat to them when they were in need of restoration.

Even talents like vampires had could be exhausted, though their magic lay more in the blood they consumed. Other creatures, such as leprechauns and púca, would need either rest, which could take time, depending on how little reserve they had left, or they could head to the wilderness for quicker renewal.

I'd never considered myself magical before, but I'd always preferred the quiet of the woods. Though now that I could identify as having supernatural abilities, my preference for the solitude of the forest made sense.

When I returned with an armful of logs, I placed them on the pile, then fed one to the ever-burning fire. Glancing around, I saw neither Joseph nor Whalen, so I wandered off to fetch more water from the river nearby.

Leaning over the bank, I marveled at its clarity, the moving stream never accommodating the frost that threatened to freeze it. A figure was reflected in it, shimmery and wavering, but I didn't recognize the face staring back at me. Terror sliced through me, and I turned to look at the man and question him, but no one was there.

I turned back to the river. I looked, but nothing was there. I blinked a few times, certain I was losing it.

Feeling all sorts of uncomfortable, I made my

way back to the men, but I was hardly away from the clearing when Whalen and Joseph were both on me in an instant. I'd been so distracted, I nearly screamed. It was Whalen who spoke first.

"What happened?" he asked.

They were the first words he'd spoken to me since I pushed him away a week ago. I couldn't say they were the first things I'd hoped to hear out of his mouth, nothing like *I've missed you terribly* or *I can't live without you,* but it was something.

I explained what happened, and the two of them exchanged a glance. For a moment, I marveled at how good they had gotten at silent communication, but I was curious to know how they knew something had happened. Before I had a chance to question him, Whalen's figure shimmered and changed.

The movement was gradual and not at the same time. The blond hair became shorter, the color bleaching into a blinding white so pure, it seemed almost unnatural. What had once been braids shimmered into short hair at the same time that his face elongated into a snout, his blue eyes changing to yellow and hands turning to paws.

Where Whalen once stood, the wolf now did, but it was fleeting, as he took off instantly. I'd never seen a wolf running up close, but I was certain that he ran faster than the average canine.

Joseph zipped to me faster than I could blink, and I hadn't even registered his arms going around me before we were flying through the woods back to our little clearing. He whistled, and both dragons were on alert. I ought to have asked him more about his experience with dragons. And probably how old he was.

Now didn't seem to be the time.

After what felt like an eternity but was probably three minutes, Whalen came in on four legs that mystically morphed into two midstride. He was wearing the same clothes he had been before he'd changed, and I added that to my list of explanations I'd need later, supposing Whalen and I were on speaking terms again.

"Nothing. They must be using magic of their own," he said to no one in particular.

Grasping the chance presented to me, I asked, "What do you mean?"

Maybe a desperate attempt, but it was the best opening I'd had in a week. If not now, then when?

"No scents, no footprints, nothing other than our own anywhere near here."

"What kind of magic would they be using?"

"Scrying, either a witch or a Druid, which means we need to move, now." He said the last with his signature growl and started moving immediately. "Joseph, take her to Amergin's. I'll grab her things and meet you there."

"B-But...," I stuttered, not sure what I was going to say. *But I don't want to leave you now, not when you're finally talking to me again.*

"No time for talking. Go," he ordered Joseph.

I was extra saddened by the lack of any sobriquet—no "sweetheart," no sarcasm, just an ordered command, and then Joseph scooped me up like an errant child and *moved.* We were at Amergin's in the span of a breath, something I was completely out of.

"Joseph...," I tried again, my mind swirling.

"Don't fret, *mo bhanríon.* He's worried is all. With good reason, too, so let's head inside without delay."

I looked at the steps, and there was the Druid, a sardonic smile on his face. *This must really chafe Whalen,* I thought as Amergin looked like the cat that got into the cream.

"Missed me?" he asked, winking at me.

I didn't deign to respond, giving him my best bored-senseless look.

"Aw, honey, come on inside. I'll keep you safe," he said, still mocking us.

Joseph didn't answer, either, but as we walked to the entrance, he moved quick as lightning at the last second and was now holding Amergin's throat within his grasp. The Druid didn't shout in alarm or cower, much to my dismay, but the ire in his eyes accepted the threat all the same.

"Touchy lot," he said when Joseph released him.

Joseph ushered me inside without another glance at Amergin.

The living room was the same, only this time, there were other items either smoking or bubbling away in the cauldron and in random bowls on the various surfaces. It smelled of herbs and made my nose itch a little.

"Who do you figure?" Joseph asked, not explaining what had happened, though I guessed Amergin knew all the same.

"There's a faction of the queen's men run by a man named Finan. Rumored to be a nasty lot. They've a host of supernatural characters in their company. But I do imagine they're on their way as we speak."

"You will keep her hidden here, and we'll draw

them away," Joseph told him more than asked, but the Druid nodded.

Whalen came through the door then, my pack in hand. He looked wild and unkempt, the fire in his eyes sizzling beneath the surface. Even with the barely contained rage, he still handled my things gently, handing them to me softly.

"We'll be back eventually. I'm not sure how long it will take to shake them, but you'll be fine with Amergin. Use your judgment," he said, addressing me to my shock and begrudging delight.

"Are you saying I would steer her in the wrong direction?" Amergin asked with feigned outrage.

For the first time, genuine panic bubbled up my throat. I wasn't thrilled with being left with Amergin to begin with, but not knowing his intentions made my stomach knot uncomfortably.

Rough fingers grabbed my chin, contrasting the light touch he did it with, and Whalen turned my face to his. There was an openness in his eyes that had been missing this past week, and I unconsciously drew a deep breath.

"He wouldn't, not even to spite me." He said the last part with a fiery glance at the Druid before returning his attention to me. "But all the same, trust your gut. He'll keep you perfectly safe, but he might be inclined to pester you."

I didn't know what to say, either too blown away by the gesture after a week of nothing or the way he was able to calm my nerves so easily. Perhaps he knew I'd been freaking out to begin with, but whatever it was, I stared back, almost too afraid to blink and break the spell he had me under.

He must have seen the silent acquiescence, because he nodded. Leaning down to me—quite far, I might say, his stature requiring it—my heart stuttered as his lips grew ever nearer. He placed them gently on my cheek, a whisper of a kiss, before he said softly to me, "Be right back."

Then he was moving, and with one firm look at Amergin, he swept out the door with conviction, a man ready to do battle. Joseph smiled at me with his usual quirk of a grin and kissed the top of my head before following Whalen.

I stood there in a daze, unsure of what to do with myself. My hands itched for Whalen, for his shoulders and his strength. And yet I also yearned for the quiet easiness that Joseph carried with him.

Amergin was neither.

He stood by one of the mortar and pestles, putting different items in before mashing them, seeming completely disinterested in me. I went ahead and put my stuff down by the overstuffed couch, then sat down on it, content to melt into it while I chewed a hole in my lip.

Not knowing how Whalen or Joseph fared was going to be the death of me.

Dread pooled in my stomach, and I tried to examine the items around the room, but to no avail. Fear and overwhelming despair sucked me under with every second that passed.

Wasn't this why I pushed Whalen away in the first place?

It was probably a sign that I was already in too deep. No turning back now, so why had I even tried?

Whalen's kiss goodbye left me thinking that was probably it. He would meet his demise before I ever got the chance to tell him how much I cared for him.

And Joseph. I'd never shown him enough appreciation for how much he'd done for me. For how much I needed him around to brighten up my days and keep me putting one foot in front of the other.

Now I sat on this couch with my chest cracked open. I was leaking emotions like a sieve, unable to patch up the wounds on full display in front of uncaring Amergin. I wanted sleep to pull me under and swallow me whole until they were safely back, but the guilt kept my eyes open.

It was my fault they were out there now, risking their lives to keep me safe. If only I hadn't gone to the river, we would be back at camp, together, silently going through the motions.

And my parents. My fault too. Maybe if I hadn't been gifted, they would be fine now too. We could be preparing to host a dinner, and they wouldn't be buried in the cold ground.

A sudden whoosh broke through my thoughts, and smoke began to fill the air. I sat up in alarm, but Amergin only sat back with an unreadable look on his face.

Images filled the room, distant but growing clearer. I could see dragons—tails and heads initially, but nothing more. Then the scene came to life.

They weren't any old dragons, though—they were my dragons, and those were my men atop them, riding with the wind. At first, I was delighted; the ability to check in on them was fascinating. However Amergin had done it, I didn't care. I was content to obtain a glimpse and be sure they were okay.

Until the scene changed.

Teeth came into view, rows of canines all yellowing and gnarly. A dragon larger still than Saoi came barreling through the sky, jaws wide open and headed straight for the green dragon. They snapped shut around his throat, blood spraying immediately. A surprised Joseph screamed, holding on to his mount for dear life.

Or maybe I was screaming, my vocal cords protesting.

Saoi and Joseph both went tumbling out of view, and I dropped to my knees as if to catch them, grasping at air. Then the other dragon turned his attention on Whalen and his mount, Neart.

I shouted for them to look, to dodge, to do anything. Whalen pulled the reins, rearing up and narrowly escaping the first attack. Neart whipped his tail, tearing into the snout of the enemy, using the moment of inattention to rake claws down its face and gouge its eyes.

But the dragon was ready, snagging one of Neart's feet in its mouth and dragging him down. Off balance, the white dragon flailed, his wings flapping hard to maintain height, which gave the opposer the chance to fling its tail right at those wings and at Whalen.

I screamed bloody murder, jumping at the image

as if to snatch Whalen right out of the sky. But it was only smoke.

Now on the ground on my hands and knees, I scrambled for the image, for a clue, for anything to show me that they were all right, that the worst hadn't happened. I was shredded. My heart had exploded right in my chest.

"What you focus on, you bring magic to," Amergin said, his voice stern and indifferent.

I hadn't the energy to care about what he said. His words fell like water through the air. There was nothing for them to grab on to, no resistance as they flew from one ear to the next. My thoughts were silent.

"Is that where you want to pour your energy?" he asked, and still I sat quietly on the ground in my own misery.

His face filled my vision, all his carefully constructed aloofness gone, his blue eyes vivid with emotion. He grabbed my chin, a parallel to the way Whalen had hours ago, or was it only minutes? Time had ceased to make sense.

Pulling gently but forcefully, he made me sit back on my haunches until he could face me truly. His eyes blazed, and his body vibrated with an intensity I hadn't seen in him before.

"Where your focus goes, the magic grows," he said, and finally his words seemed to stick somewhere in my consciousness.

"Was... was it not real?" I questioned, the syllables thick and mumbled through my emotions.

"It will be if you keep harping on it. I once let fear control me, too, and my worst ones came true. Don't make the same mistakes as me," he said, getting up and walking away from me in one smooth motion, life lesson over. "I made tea," he called over a shoulder.

I was too dumbfounded to move at first. Then the anger hit.

"What the hell was it, then?" I shouted. I was so mad, I wanted to flip one of his stupid tables, but I restrained myself.

"A possibility. There're endless possibilities, you'll find, but the ones that come true are often the ones you put your attention on."

"What does that mean? Are they okay? What is wrong with you?" I spat out rapidly, stumbling over the words in my haste.

I straightened the mess I'd made of my hair, my clothes, and my face as he calmly poured hot water into two steaming mugs. They were earthenware, thick and heavy, durable things. He handed me one, a flicker of something passing over his face that I couldn't read in time.

I took it, hands trembling and heart racing, but I was glad for something to do with them even if I wouldn't drink it—not before I witnessed him take a sip.

He took his sweet time, of course.

"It's not poison," he said, not looking at me but at a spot on the wall to his right.

"A potion, then," I said with certainty.

"Neither. Only tea. I prefer it strong and plain. I hope you find it to your liking."

I think I growled then, frustration bubbling over.

He took the mug back out of my hand and gingerly sipped from my cup before gargling and swallowing it audibly. As he handed it back to me, I saw some of the mischief in his eyes again, but this time his gaze was also warmhearted.

"Drink, please," he requested softly.

I obliged, taking a gentle sip. The warmth was an elixir of its own. Heating without burning, soothing my frayed nerves and sore throat before spreading through my veins like a summer's day.

"What is this?" I asked, sipping again eagerly, craving the comfort and peace it doled out.

"A blend of ashwagandha, lavender, chamomile, some black tea, too, since it's early yet. Good?"

"It's heavenly," I said truthfully before inhaling deeply from the mug. "Now, please explain."

He smiled gently, eyes crinkling at the corners.

"Sorry for the shock," he said, and I thought he was genuine.

"It's okay," I said, not sure if I meant it or not yet, but I would say anything for him to talk more.

"I showed you only a glimpse into a future that could exist. Simple magic, born from your imagination. But a reality that could exist if you let it."

"I don't understand."

"As Druids, we don't receive the gift of insight or the infinite wisdom on what route is best, but we do get the ability to help weave the future. It's difficult to explain. Do you know how sometimes you know things? Things you ought not to? Intuition, your gut, the gods guiding you?"

I'd never discussed that with anyone before. The way signs always seemed to point me in the direction I should be going. Or where I should definitely not be going.

I nodded for him to continue.

"We're touched, gifted, energetically aligned. I'm not sure what to call it, but the possibilities we see gain traction when we focus on them. They become reality because we cultivate them. These tools and techniques around the room help us to navigate these paths we see and the pieces as a whole. And our job is to nourish the favorable ones and hinder the other ones."

He looked at me to be sure I was following. I nodded hesitantly, knowing what he was saying but not necessarily why.

"The scene I showed you before was the one you were focusing on, the one you were bringing into reality. Doom and gloom, death and destruction. It could very well happen if you home in on it.

"Whalen is fine. Joseph and the dragons are fine right now. But you need to learn that your thoughts and feelings can dictate this situation. They can alter it and create something you either want or don't want. It's your choice.

"I needed to shock you only to teach you. I do apologize for such a harsh lesson," he said a little apologetically.

I breathed deeply, filling my lungs with air I didn't realize they needed. A stuttering, sniffling one, but afterward, I felt the tension in me release a few notches.

"As we train, you'll understand what I mean."

I took him at his word, but I had so many questions for him now.

I asked the most pressing one first. "So, they're fine?"

"Aye, I'll show them to you," he said, motioning toward a clear crystal on one of the tables.

Swirling his hands around the rough ball, he recited a few words. Green and white eddied before coming into view, and then the four of them were racing through the skies. No evil dragon on their tails, and no clouds to hide one either.

"They're doing fine. See?"

I nodded, biting my lip. *How could I believe that this was the true vision?*

"What?" he asked, sensing my hesitation.

"But what about my parents? I didn't focus on that," I whispered softly instead, afraid to voice the words.

"Maybe not you, but perhaps someone else had. But this is all much more random than you would think. We control aspects of it all but not the whole story. There are too many variables."

I nodded again, this time because of the lump in my throat.

"Drink," he ordered, and I obeyed, a weariness settling over me.

"How long will they be gone?" I asked suddenly. I thought it would be only an hour, but the reality hit me with a vengeance.

"Days, at least," he answered, headed to another room as he spoke.

I followed at a distance, unsure of whether I should or not. If he'd been walking to his bedroom, I would have died of embarrassment. I wasn't sure I would mind following him to his bedroom, but certainly not yet. I hardly knew him.

Amergin was handsome, there was no denying it. His brown hair flowed luxuriously to his broad and muscled shoulders. Round, heavy curls framed his sculpted face in waves as wild and free as he was not.

He kept a thick beard, surprisingly neat despite the length. His perfectly square jaw was visible beneath it and his broad high cheeks above it. White caught my eye at its edge, mottled skin peeking over the top of the coating of hair and into his hairline, a poorly healed scar.

I was surprised I hadn't seen it before, but I hadn't been this close to him yet or paying much attention to him either. I wondered what caused it. The striking color of it zigzagged a little but was clean, as if made by a sword. A thin, long nose sat to the left of the scar, perfectly straight as a blade.

But most striking were his eyes. Bright as the blue sky. So clear and endless, you could get lost in them. And when his mood changed, so did they, turning stormy like the sea surrounding us.

Luckily, he led me to the kitchen, a cozy thing containing a wood stove and some cabinets and little else. A pot sat on top of the hob, something bubbling in it smelling rich with herbs and spices.

Seeing him in the small space made his frame even bigger than I had realized. Though he lacked the bulk that Whalen had, he was equally tall and broad but leaner. He reached back to tie up a section of his hair, and the sleeves of his cloak fell back to reveal intricate tattoos covering every inch of skin, creeping down his hands.

"Protection," he said simply, stirring the stew before tasting a steaming bite.

He must have thought it needed something, because he added a few more spices to it and stirred again. He took off his robe and hung it on a hook before opening the door to the stove and reaching in with a bare arm.

Beneath the robe, he wore a sleeveless under- shirt and loose linen pants that accentuated his narrow waist and well-defined abs. Where Whalen was a broadsword, Amergin was a spear.

He pulled out a loaf of bread with a pair of towels and placed it on top of the stove where it would stay warm but no longer cook. The crust looked golden brown and delicious, and I marveled at this gruff man in front of me.

He put another log in and stoked the flames higher. The silence that filled the air wasn't uncomfortable. He was likely as used to quiet as I was.

"Are you hungry?" he asked when he was finished, wiping his hands on his pants to clear the ashes.

"No, thank you," I said, sipping from my tea some more.

He chugged his before slamming it down. I tried not to look at his lean muscles as he did so, the way the bottom of his shirt rose to reveal a sliver of skin covered in tattoos and a dusting of hair.

I failed. Miserably.

He replaced his robe and motioned toward the living room. The twinkle in his eye told me he'd caught my lingering gaze, but thankfully he didn't bring it up.

In the living room, he moved toward the table with the mortar and pestle. He grabbed different herbs and gestured for me to stand in front of the bowl. I did, placing my tea down and quirking an eyebrow at him.

"Think of good things. It can be about the two of them in general or anything that makes you smile," he said, looking at me intently.

"Do I have to smile?" I asked, not knowing why it made me feel uncomfortable, like he was one of those men who always asked women to smile—the sleazy ones who made my skin crawl.

Instead, he was the one who smiled, giving a soft laugh.

"No. Please don't, in fact. Just think positive thoughts so we can set the right intention for the spell I'm going to show you how to do."

It seemed strange, but I rolled with it. The trouble was, now that there was pressure to think of something positive, I was coming up blank.

Nothing, not a thing crossed my mind. I squinched my eyes closed tight and tried to conjure up images of Whalen, but it seemed as if I'd forgotten his face. I tried thinking of Joseph and his easy comfort but was met with more noth-ingness.

Finally giving up, I looked at Amergin with exas-peration. Those piercing blue eyes were staring at me with such intensity that I thought I swallowed audibly, but he blinked, and it was gone.

"I've got nothing," I said, recovering slightly.

"Let me see," he said, rounding the table.

Unsure what he was doing, I tracked his movement and gasped when he grabbed my hips in both hands, backing me into the table. His hands swallowed the swell of each of them, and his heat seeped into mine at the closeness of his body. He leaned down slowly, and I gripped the table, lust coursing through me at his boldness.

The thought of his lips on mine made all types of feelings run through me. I thought of Whalen then, of his warning and his feelings. Would he even be upset if I were to become involved with Amergin? Or did he not care enough about me to begin with?

"Have you got something now?" he whispered in my ear before backing away altogether, leaving me floundering at the suddenness.

Anger replaced the raging hormones as I realized he'd done it only to get a rise out of me. I didn't know if I was mad at him or myself for it working.

"Good, use that," he said, seeing the fire in my eyes.

"The anger? I thought I was supposed to think something positive," I snapped.

He wasn't fazed, not in the slightest. Instead, I was fairly sure he ate it up, loving the controversy.

"Any strong emotion will do for this to start," he said with a roguish wink that had me clenching my jaw. "Now, think about what you want to have happen to them, their safe return, what your reunion might be, how they'll look, what they might say...," he said, trailing off at the end.

I did then, but for reasons I couldn't explain, images of Whalen and Amergin kept flashing in my mind. Each of them kissing me in turn, being content to share me. Joseph crossed my mind as well, but I wasn't sure how he could fit in that dynamic, if at all.

I broke the train of thought before I got too deep into it. My attraction to both men, or perhaps all of them, was not the point of the exercise right now. And besides, I had a clan to return to and lead. I could hardly have multiple paramours and be taken seriously.

Oisin wouldn't be interested in sharing me either. And then there was the worry that they may only be interested in me for my family and the power I held. Or worse yet, sex and that alone. Though to be truthful, I almost didn't care about it at the moment.

Almost.

"Have you got an idea yet?" he asked, and by his tone, I knew he was aware that I did not.

Focusing again, I saw it then. The two of them walking through the door here, maybe dirty and tired but hale and hearty. I could go up to each of them and hug them tightly, feel ensconced in their embrace and indulge myself in their smell.

Joseph would undoubtedly say something soothing and kind. Whalen might have a bite of sarcasm that would make me laugh or blush, usually both. And the weight of terror and danger would be removed, and we could be safe and sound again. Amergin, too, his wicked smile turning soft at the removal of the pressure he kept on himself.

If only I knew why he looked so weighed down all the time. There was more in his eyes than just the loss, something that clung to him like a shroud, adding a tightness to his mouth that deepened when he didn't think I was paying attention.

He must have sensed I had what I needed, because he began pouring herbs into the bowl, the sound tinkling in my ears. I opened my eyes to find his boring into mine again, that same strong emotion in them I couldn't pinpoint.

"Use the pestle," he said, grabbing more ingredients.

We worked quietly beside each other for probably an hour. He would mumble words in the ancient tongue as he did so, and soon the air was electric. My anger turned to a feeling of joy like I had never known growing in the pit of my stomach, as if this was the most exciting thing I had ever done, though all I did was keep grinding.

Eventually, he deemed the work worthy, and I looked at him to find him glowing. Not just his expression but Amergin himself was sort of glowing, his body strangely backlit amid a dark cloud surrounding him.

"Grab the crystals," he said, and I walked to the shelves before realizing he hadn't told me which one.

"You already know," he insisted, and I gave him a long look before grabbing the white one that had called to me before.

For Joseph, I found an earth-toned stone that was as homey as he was. The white one screamed passion and wilderness in my other hand, and I coveted it slightly. There were the black and red ones from earlier that I craved, but something told me not to touch them. Not yet.

I walked back to the table but stopped midway to turn back. Scanning the wall, I noticed one that reminded me of hardened smoke, gray and mysterious. It felt like holding a hurricane, magnificent and deadly but so beautiful at the same time.

I handed them to Amergin, and his eyes were quizzical and skeptical at first, but then they shuttered, and he went to work.

Taking each stone in turn, he passed them over the mixture. His words sent shivers down my spine, and I wanted to hold each one in my hand, to turn them over and examine them.

After placing a different stone in three spots around the bowl, he put a rune carved on a plain stone in the last space. The knots were intricate and stunning, and the magic from the stone pulsed through the room, steady as a drum.

Amergin spoke with a flourish then. Ending the ritual with a feather, he held one end to the flame on the table before placing it in the bowl. The ingredients sparked and fizzled, making me gasp in awe.

"What was that?" I whispered. The silence was taut, like a balloon about to pop.

"Protection spell for them. You did well," he said, a slight smirk showing me his thoughts.

I blushed, unsure of how to feel about him encroaching on my personal space. Perhaps that was what Whalen had meant when he said Amergin would play tricks on me.

Damn it, but my body betrayed me. It hadn't been my intention, but something about the man had my blood heating up.

"Thank you," I said meekly, trying and failing to put more confidence into my voice.

He genuinely smiled then, and the force of it blew me away. Blue eyes twinkled like the night sky, and his smile was the sun. The scar on his face wrinkled aggressively, and it only made him more devastating. Dangerously so.

"I have to find more firewood. Make yourself comfortable. I'll be back later."

It took too long for his words to register. My brain knew it, but it was too focused on the change in his demeanor. Gods help me but he was apparently charming.

"How long will you be gone?" I asked as he was nearly out the hidden door.

"A few hours. Try not to get into trouble, will you?" he admonished with a wink, and then he was gone.

Thank the gods.

I stood there numbly until the heat of him washed away and the memory of his smile faded.

This was the epitome of trouble.

A CLAMORING SOUND CAME FROM THE DOOR, AND I jumped out of my skin, unsheathing a knife on my hip. Holding it at the ready, I relaxed when I noticed Amergin coming in, arms laden with firewood.

I ambled over to help him, putting the knife away. I made room near the hearth for the wood, grabbing logs as he handed them to me to stack in the cubby tucked into the stone. Plenty of wood was already in there, but I didn't mention it. He seemed to be a well-prepared kind of guy.

When we were done, he grabbed my wrist, pushing it up and down.

"You want to go this way," he said and again started with my wrist in the up position and then pushed it down. "Not this." This time he held my wrist at my hip and pulled it up.

Flabbergasted, I looked at him like the psychopath I thought he was. The same magnanimous smile lit his face before he grabbed the knife out of the sheath at my waist and showed me the second motion first, the knife pointed up the way I'd held it before.

Again he pulled my hand up, toward his stomach, and I recoiled in horror.

"This way is easy to block," he said, putting his forearm on top of mine as if pushing me away, "and easier to break your wrist if you hit bone, which is more likely this way. What you want to do—" Now he turned the knife the other way in my palm until it pointed toward me before he pushed my elbow up. "—is hold it this way and slash down into my shoulder. I can't block it as easily, and you're using your stronger muscles this way, so you won't hurt yourself."

I tried to say something, anything, but I was gasping like a fish out of water. His one hand still gripped my wrist, the knife's point above his heart. The other was still poised in a feeble block, the forearm more exposed and less effective from that angle. I'd had sword and archery training but less hand-to-hand experience, always reminded that in battle, my best defense would be a good offense. I would likely not best a man like Amergin if he got too close.

"I'd rather not stab you," I said breathlessly, captivated by his big blue eyes.

"You say that now," he replied with a wink, but the defenses shored up in his eyes as if he fully believed I would hurt him one day. I wondered what it was like to have to remain so closed off from the world, but he was already gone.

"Hungry now?" was all he said.

I was, and he looked back to see my nod. Following him to the kitchen, I stopped to mark a page in the book I had grabbed in his absence. After exploring the small space a little, it had only been natural to choose one.

I had marveled at the stones, feathers, runes, and other magical objects before the temptation to look at his room became too great. I'd tiptoed to it as if the walls would tell on me, and I peeked my head through to find more of the same. Odd books were strewn on the bedside table, and the objects hung above his bed were seemingly innocuous but surely held power of some sort.

He was disorganized but not sloppy. There was clearly a method to his madness.

The bed was simple and unadorned other than the crosses and knots that decorated the wall behind it. It was unmade, and the gray sheets looked worn and haphazard, as if he always slept in fits and starts.

I'd crept away as silently as I had gone, curiosity soothed momentarily. The book I'd grabbed detailed oral histories that had been written down over generations, and my body screamed with delight that dozens, if not hundreds, or even thousands of people who had come before me had sat and listened to the same tales. My ancestors heard them well before me, and now here I was, reveling in the same story.

It had kept my rapt attention until Amergin came barreling through the door. My fingers itched to open it again, but a handsome man was making me dinner, which made me feel another itch that I yearned to scratch even more. It often seemed like I was forever torn between reality and fantasy.

Making it to the archway to the kitchen, I watched as he grabbed bowls and forks from the cabinet tucked away in the corner. The setup was truly amazing—almost too perfect. There had to be magic involved.

He lived in a cave, so the smoke from the fires should be suffocating, but the air was warm and fresh as if ventilated somewhere I couldn't see. The dark wasn't absolute either. Though candles helped light the space, they weren't big enough, nor were there enough of them, to warrant the brightness of the space. And by some grace of the gods, I had not seen a bug yet.

He ladled stew into a bowl and handed it to me, the warmth seeping into my hands flawlessly, the earthenware thick and solid. He cut off two hunks of bread from the loaf he'd made and placed them on a plate, then indicated for me to head back toward the living room.

At a snap of his fingers, the mess was gone. Every table and couch was set to rights, and I wondered why he had left it that way to begin with. Pulling out a chair in what must be the dining room, he gallantly motioned for me to sit. I took the seat with a bemused look at him, and he answered with one of his own.

After pushing my chair in, he did another little wave, and lit candles appeared on the table alongside fresh flowers, soft music filling the air. He sauntered into the kitchen and returned with his bowl and a pitcher of water. He placed his bowl down, and then he started pouring water right onto the table. A glass suddenly appeared to catch it at the last second.

I laughed despite myself, a grin lighting my face. His charm was addictive, and I was getting myself into trouble the more I let him pull me in. The trouble was, I couldn't help myself. I was already craving more. And he knew it.

"Clever," I said as he repeated the trick with his glass.

"I aim to please."

I harrumphed—to his delight, it seemed, as he gave me a wicked grin. He was fun. Much too fun.

Digging into my stew, I groaned in ecstasy. It was better than it had any right to be. The meat was tender and lean, the vegetables still had a bite to them, and the whole dish was seasoned exquisitely.

"Glad you're taking pleasure in it," he said, echoing his previous statement.

"It's delicious," I said, trying not to shovel it in my face like the savage I could be sometimes.

"I grow the vegetables a ways south of here. The grains too. Venison from the woods. Spices too."

"You're a wizard," I joked, speaking to a Druid.

He laughed, a hearty one that wasn't warranted, considering the quip was mediocre at best. But the fire in his eyes spoke volumes.

"I could say the same about you," he said simply.

An undertone marked the words, though, one I pondered as I continued to eat. He looked at me as if he'd like to feast on me, and I blushed wildly as I averted my eyes.

Guilt hit my stomach a second later. Here I was, flirting ostentatiously with Whalen's enemy as if he weren't out there defending me against enemies both seen and not as my parents rotted in their graves and other children were made orphans too.

Suddenly my appetite waned. I still ate, knowing I needed the nourishment and not wanting to be rude, and it wasn't as if the food wasn't delectable. Only now a pit was growing in my stomach, a weed I couldn't pluck out and snuff.

A warm hand covered mine on the table, and I flinched, nearly pulling away from him. Only politeness kept my hand beneath his as I peeked at him.

Concern colored his face, making him seem younger and older at the same time. I worried at my lip, unsure of how to react to his kindness.

"It will all work out," he said, a kind of proverb

you say when you're not sure what the outcome will be.

"Work out how is the question," I responded.

"Ah, well, honey, that's another conversation entirely."

"You keep calling me that. And it's the only conversation that matters."

"I don't disagree with you, but it's not one that ever ends, is it?"

No, it wasn't.

"Why do you call me 'honey'?"

He chuckled easily, weighing his answer before he spoke again.

"Because you're the pot of gold. But to have you, a man needs to climb the tallest tree, fend off the bears, and potentially be stung to death before he ever gets a taste. And if he does, it will be the sweetest thing he's ever tried, I have no doubt."

*Gods strike me where I stand. Sit. Whatever I'm doing right now, because I can't even say.*

"You are definitely a wizard," I repeated, mostly to myself.

"You haven't seen anything yet, honey," he said with a wink to unclothe every woman in the surrounding towns.

But I saw it then. The charm and the jokes were

meant to disarray, to dislodge the depression, to give my mind something else to cling to. If I hadn't known it before, I saw it now in the warmth in his eyes. The understanding.

He let go of my hand then, and we ate in companionable silence for a while. The bread was crunchy on the outside and soft and doughy inside, rich with grains that lent it a nuttiness that was heavenly.

I wanted to say something, anything, to thank him, but the words wouldn't come out. It was as if I couldn't let them because then I would be acknowledging the darkness within me. And if I did, it would only grow in power until it consumed me.

Daring a look at him, I saw that it was all reflected back at me. His eyes were a whirlpool, the chasms alluring and seductive. I wanted to dive in and drown myself.

He blinked then, a sharp slicing motion, and the blue depths were clear again. So smooth, they became glass, cutting off the world that existed behind them.

"If you've no more appetite, honey, I can show you around."

"Outside?" I queried.

"Not yet, no. The threat is too close still. I can

show you inside to the other rooms in here. You've one of your own you can bring your things to and settle in."

I worried at my lip again. How long was I going to be here? And why didn't he show me before he so suddenly went to fetch more firewood? More questions for later.

"I'm sorry. I lost my appetite," I said, admitting defeat.

"Not to worry. I haven't," he said, pulling my bowl to him and finishing the last of my food.

I giggled again. He did it with such enthusiasm that I was disarmed.

"You said it yourself, this is delicious," he said around a mouthful of food in a way that had me smiling bigger.

There was such an intimacy to eating someone else's food that had me both baffled and fascinated. But the undeniable joy his behavior wrung out of me made me see him in a different light.

"It is," I agreed and drank from my magical glass.

I examined it for anything to explain the way it suddenly appeared but could find nothing. Tapping my fingernails against the surface proved it was real glass, but where it had come from remained a mystery.

"There's nothing to do with the glass, but eventually I can show you how to do parlor tricks of your own."

"But what you do isn't magic, is it?"

"Isn't it? And it's what *we* do, honey."

I gave an exaggerated eye roll.

"Do you need to call me that every time?"

"Oh, yes, it's a requirement, honey," he said with another devilish grin.

I'd be lying if I said I didn't enjoy it. I mostly feared Whalen wouldn't. Or Oisin.

Damn, my head was spinning with these men. What was a girl supposed to do, anyway? In an ideal —albeit crazy—world, I would keep them all. One for every kind of mood.

Whalen to challenge me, Amergin to dazzle me, Joseph to ground me, and Oisin—I didn't know what he did for me yet, but I'd wager he inspired me.

I wish Whalen and Joseph were here now, safely ensconced in this hideaway with us. We could forget the world existed, if only for a little while.

I stood up and was grabbing the dishes to clean in the sink when Amergin's hand landed on mine. He didn't have the impish look to him for once as he snapped his fingers, and the bowls and cutlery were clean as a whistle. With a second flick of his fingers, they were gone.

"Handy" was all I said.

If I'd known I could do this, I wouldn't have wasted all that time scrubbing the dishes at my house while I was trying and failing to hide from Whalen. What I would have done with the extra time, I didn't know, but I would have preferred to have found out.

Truthfully, had I known about my abilities, I would have spent more time seeking out the White Wolf. So it may have been for the better that I hadn't been able to.

"Ready?" he asked, standing up and holding out an arm for me.

Leave it to him to be the epitome of a gentleman. Taking his arm delicately, I tried not to moan at the hard muscles his robes concealed. How badly I wanted to feel his skin and trace every tattoo with my tongue.

*Don't think that!* I scolded myself.

For heaven's sake, I was blushing like a maiden here, thinking about every inch of those tattoos. I wondered if they were *everywhere*. I hoped they were. I imagined Whalen's tattoos then, trying to see in my mind's eye if they were similar to Amergin's.

*Oh no, please let him say something before I blurt my thoughts out loud. I need help.*

Zero chance he didn't feel the heat radiating off me at his touch—I was damn near broadcasting. I should simply tell him to join me in my bedroom when we got there at this rate.

Then a horrible thought occurred to me. If he could wash the dishes with a snap of his fingers, could he beguile me the way he was? Against my will?

Whalen told me to be cautious with him. Was my instinct telling me that he was persuading my thoughts? Could he control my emotions? Or was this me trying to downplay my visceral reaction to him, attempting to explain away this immense attraction?

However, if I was honest with myself, it may be that I was protecting my mind from all the horror I'd faced recently and all the anxiety still swirling around inside me. And what a good distraction he was.

The wave ebbed again, and I was no longer riding on a high. Now I was spinning, plummeting to the earth, and I was about to crash headlong into the rocks.

Where was Whalen? Was he still okay? What was he facing now as I shamelessly groped Amergin's bicep?

Self-hatred came next. What weak and frivolous woman was I that I was getting swept up in this flirtation with any of them when I was supposed to be helping save others from harm?

I knew we'd made it to the room because Amergin stopped and opened the door with a flourish. This time, a real door was set into the rock wall, curved to match the natural archway and protect the integrity of the stone. There were runes carved in the wood with a rich lacquer finish over it.

"Yew?" I asked, recognizing the grain.

"Aye. An ancient tree felled in a churchyard a long time ago, and I wouldn't see the thing be wasted. Powerful magic in yews," he said, touching the door with reverence.

"It's beautiful."

"Fitting," he said with a wink at me that had me blushing and looking away. "It's late now, so I'll leave you to it. The bathroom is across the way, so it's a short walk. I'm down at the end if you have need of me. And there's a window you might peek through. It's a sight to see, even in the dark."

"Thank you," I said, releasing his arm.

He did another snap, and my things thumped behind me like a sack of potatoes. I needed to learn how to do that!

"Well, have a good night, honey. If you're scared, you can always come and crawl into my bed." He smiled suggestively before grabbing my hand and kissing it gently, making me swoon all over again.

"Keep dreaming, *honey*."

"Oh, I will. Sweet dreams to you, too, dear," he said, closing the door behind him.

I called a good night to him with an eye roll in my voice. Truth be told, now that I was alone, I was a little frightened. Not that I was ready to crawl into bed with Amergin, but I hadn't slept without guards in a while. Both Joseph and Whalen had kept watch on the road, and I supposed before them, there had been Evelyn.

To be so alone now was uncomfortable.

Shaking off the feeling, I went to the window to see what all the fuss was about. Black blanketed the view outside, illuminated by millions of shining stars and a moon that hung low and bright enough to cast the sea in its brilliant light. Waves crashed against the shore in a staccato rhythm, and the rocks they broke against spewed the salt water into stunning rays of white against the night sky.

The scene was breathtaking.

Mountains and cliffs loomed beyond, marrying earth and ocean in a union that was dazzling. Two great powers clashing, neither side winning nor losing, equally great in strength and size.

I didn't know how long I sat and watched the spectacle before me. Though it was long enough to ponder the dichotomies in my own life and mind.

# CHAPTER TWELVE

Days passed in a monotony of lessons and stress. Each day I wore a path at the end of my bed, waiting for news of Whalen or obsessing over the lack of it.

Amergin showed me how to read runes and cards, to make hexes and potions, how to channel my energy. But the bundle of nerves that ate away my insides didn't dissipate. Rather, it eroded what was left of my sensibility until I was a walking eggshell, ready to fall and break at the slightest breeze.

He did his best to cajole me with his continuous barbs and unrestrained flirtation, but they had since fallen flat. I was wasted in worry and unease.

"You're not even trying, Emer." Amergin's voice

cut through my misery only to plunge me further into it.

I wasn't trying. Heavens help me, but I had nothing to give. There was no fire left, no embers, only cold ashes in an empty hearth.

"If you want to help them, you can, but not this way," he said again.

"I *can't*," I stressed again, the same excuse I kept using.

It fell flat, even to my ears. But there were no other words for the listlessness plaguing me.

"You won't. There's a difference," he said with real anger this time.

That had been the trend over the past few days. I had excelled at the lessons at first, but worry and fear led to a void I couldn't fight. In one corner of my mind, I recognized my brain's defense mechanism of shutting down when I was too overwhelmed. But it didn't mean I could do anything about it.

No amount of threats or punishments could rile me—not lately. Nor for lack of trying on Amergin's part either. I was numb.

No magic happened that way, I knew. But maybe I was tired of fighting.

Amergin stomped off, another thing that had become normal.

Today we were working on a potion that would give the user strength and vitality beyond the norm.

The irony wasn't lost on me.

A knock sounded at the door. The dwelling being well off the beaten path, I'd almost have been less surprised if a bell rang to alert us of someone's presence.

Amergin was on his way to grab it when the door opened on its own. My heart was in my throat, and I was praying Whalen and Joseph were back to embrace me and take away this haunting shroud.

Instead, a large man with dark auburn hair, dark eyes, and an ominous presence walked through the door. He seemed to suck all the air out of the room with the authority oozing out of him.

"Ruad," Amergin said, not impolitely.

"A word," he said to him, nodding at me in acknowledgment.

I took the cue to excuse myself, and I averted my attention to the task at hand. The potion was meant to aid a Druid's abilities more than anything else. According to Amergin, this was how I would gain the strength to manipulate objects and weave expert spells.

As if tapping into my inner strength and hidden knowledge was going to make a difference somehow. He warned that it couldn't enhance anything that wasn't innate in a person, only awaken what existed.

This morning, we'd gathered different herbs and objects from the surrounding forest and seascape in the rising sun to imbue them with the same qualities. Once we'd finished, we did a morning ritual that included thanking the Earth for its bounty, the sun for its rays, and the magic for lending us its power.

I was finding life with Amergin included many rituals and practices. In the morning, he woke me before the first light, and then we would exercise and prepare our minds for the day, including a cold dip in the ocean before returning to the cave, as I called it.

He would say thanks to the food he prepared, the animals who gave their lives for ours, and the fruits and vegetables that sustained us. In his belief system, all of life was sacred, the apple no less important than the housefly or the deer, certainly no less than us.

In truth, I had benefitted greatly from his opinions and the order he brought to my life. On one hand, I was perhaps the most in tune I had ever been, savoring every moment as it flitted by in a sequence of events that led one to another.

On the other, I couldn't stop being obsessed with the things I couldn't control, worrying and projecting my fears onto the future in a way he had informed me was dooming it.

I tried to clear my mind as he'd said, but now I could only focus on the deep voices emanating from the other room. There was undoubtedly a spell put on them preventing me from overhearing, because they were hardly too far from my ears for me to hear them.

Frustrated with my inability to eavesdrop, I looked at the items again and grabbed a few. When I concentrated, I could feel the whisper of something ethereal in the objects, a touch of magic and substance.

Thanking the sage was natural to me. On some level, I always felt that way. Perhaps a lesson taught by my father that I couldn't remember when or how, but subconsciously, I did it with everything.

The way I thanked the spirits of the animals we would hunt, and the forest for the food we would forage, and the crops for their harvest. I wasn't sure it was cognizant, but my parents had done it as well. Sometimes audibly but not always, like a sensation.

The trees spoke, the plants whispered, and every animal communicated if you paid attention. I had never thought that was something *more*; I thought it was natural to everyone, not just me or Druids.

Losing myself in the feel of the herbs, I jumped when the men reappeared. The two shook hands, but when the man named Ruad approached me, I balked a little.

"Don't let him ruin the experience for you. What you're doing makes a difference," he said, and something eased in me at his words.

Truthfully, I wondered if he'd used a spell on me, because I was ignited with more determination than I'd had before. But I hardly had time to ask him as he strode for the door, a man on a mission.

In reality, I might feel more embarrassed at my own selfishness than anything else. A weariness marked his countenance that moved me in a way I wasn't prepared for.

"Thank you anyway, Amergin," he said as he walked out the door. "Take care, Emer," he said to me with one final wink before he was gone.

"How did he know my name?" I asked, perplexed.

"He knows a great deal more than your name, honey."

"Well, what was that, though?"

"You'll begin to experience more of that as your abilities grow stronger—more visitors, more poor souls asking for your help. The same way you made your way to me, other beings do too."

"Who was he?"

"Ruad, the God of Knowledge," he said without elaboration.

"Then what does he need with you?"

"He needs me as much as, if not more than, anyone else. His magic allows him to see all, but not everything he sees comes to be."

"I don't understand. Why does that mean he needs you?"

He sighed heavily and debated a moment.

"It's a long story, a long history, one Ruad has with a woman he loves. It's never a happy visit."

"Then why does he still come?"

"Why are you moping around here? Because you care about Whalen. The difference is, you're not sure if you're in love with him. Ruad has loved her for centuries, and nothing will change that. So he shows up and asks me for guidance, for a different answer than I can give him."

"How do you know?" I gasped, and he caught what I meant.

"Because I loved a woman as Ruad loves his own. And my story isn't nearly as happy as his. It's not difficult to see in your eyes that you have feelings for Whalen."

"His story is happy?"

Then he laughed, a broken rasp that didn't reach his eyes.

"Happier than mine," he said, and I could see his jaw working with pent-up emotions.

"What do you mean?"

"At least he still gets her. He never did her wrong. I can't say the same for myself."

I would ask for more, but his tone wasn't offering room for explanation. Indeed, he even moved back to the table I was working at and gestured pointedly.

"If you want to have a happier story than mine, I suggest you start working," he said, his face blank.

My depression felt petulant then, and I had to suck up the rest of it, lest I worsen it. Whatever Amergin was, he had been nice to me, if a little sarcastic.

I bit my lip, worrying about his story, wondering about it. Was his recent lack of sympathy with me because he had made the same mistake I was currently making?

I didn't have time to think about it now, though, not while he was awaiting me.

Throwing myself into the task at hand, I shut out the noise in my head. Amergin's instructions were stated with precision, and all emotion was drained from him.

I followed dutifully, even working up a modicum of, dare I say, hope into it. Maybe the feeling was the fear of failing or a gentle nudge from the gentleman who'd visited, but I could work up a little more positivity now than I could before.

The trouble with hope was that it was fickle. And the last thing I wanted was to allow myself to dream, only for those dreams to be dashed to smithereens at the end of it all. But following that logic, I should never dare to dream about anything. So, for Whalen and Joseph's sake, I could scrounge up a little shred of it. Because ultimately, it was for them that I needed to do this, not for myself.

Eventually, perhaps, it could be for me too. Currently, I had to grasp what I could.

The potion was finished with a flourish, and Amergin made me pause and pray over it before imbibing it. A simple prayer said in the old tongue.

"Go maire bhur laethanta's bhur dtrioblóidí gann, Beannacht Dé go léir anuas oraibh. Go mbeadh an tsíocháin ionat. Go mbeadh bhur gcroí láidir. Go bhfaighfeá a bhfuil uait pé áit a n-imíonn tú." He said the words slowly, allowing me to repeat them line by line.

The saying went, "May your days be many and your troubles be few. May all God's blessings descend upon you. May peace be within you. May your heart be strong. May you find what you're seeking wherever you roam."

It was a beautiful saying; the sentiment filled me with a longing I didn't realize I needed so desperately. Tears sprang from my eyes as the words rang true deep within me, reminding me how precious this life was and how few got to enjoy the fruits of it.

When I looked at Amergin, he indicated for me to drink the potion, and I did. I could immediately feel the liquid course through me like fire, burning away the emotions no longer serving me and filling me with a renewed sense of purpose.

Part of me wanted to sob, and the other part wanted to sing and dance. It seemed as if I were mourning what was, yet I was also excited for what could be. There was a headiness to the feeling, as if I were both the most important thing in the universe and, at the same time, I recognized my insignificance in the grand scheme of the world.

Amergin smiled then, a proud one, the joy meeting his eyes for once. He grasped my hand, squeezing it before getting up.

"Well, then, let's go to work."

---

THE NEXT FEW DAYS WERE A BLUR OF DIFFERENT POTIONS and spells. He taught me how to find the herbs he used for most of his spells and where he sourced a lot of the other items. There were apparently a lot of locals who would come to sell their wares to him, and they directed lots of salesmen his way, too, if they had something Amergin was likely to buy.

Of course, none of them actually knew where he resided, but rather he would know when to show up at the market for more items. Generally, he said he made the trip monthly to one market or another in some of the smaller towns and surrounding villages. But if not, he had his farm, and some of the ones he trusted most would find him while he tended the animals and crops.

I was currently working on a parlor trick, as he called it, but a useful one. I'd been trying to light the fire in the hearth with only my mind for hours now, and I was ready to light the whole place on fire instead out of frustration.

"The more you try to control it, the less you're able to. It has to be natural. You have to allow the magic to flow through you. Anger is only blocking your ability more," he said for probably the hundredth time.

"But isn't anger akin to fire? It should be useful to it, not detrimental."

"Honey, the idea is to be at one with your abilities. We are meant to be impartial sorts of people; emotions aren't supposed to play a role here."

"Because you're so peaceful and at ease," I said, rolling my eyes.

"With my magic, yes. The rest of it? Well, there's a reason I sequestered myself as far away from civilization as I possibly could."

"So, do as you say, not as you do. Got it."

He laughed then, an easy one that made me glad. They were becoming more and more commonplace as opposed to the bitter ones that plagued him before.

"Well, in this instance, the master would love it if his protégé surpassed him. I've made many mistakes, honey. I'd rather not see you repeat them."

I nodded then, a fair assessment. In truth, I'd

prefer to avoid making any mistakes. Not when I knew those mistakes could cost people everything.

"Won't be happening anytime soon, it seems," I said, indicating my failure to light the fire.

"Let's try something else, then."

He grabbed my hand and nudged me back toward the table. This time he pulled out the crystal and a few other artifacts for scrying.

"Now, take these in your hands and focus on the magic inside you, and I'll direct it this time."

I nodded and did as he said. He closed his eyes for a moment and motioned for me to throw the objects as he'd shown me before.

Placing a hand over the crystal, he waved it, mumbling words I couldn't hear. The clear stone turned milky before scenes popped up, very similar to how he'd shown me Whalen and Joseph before, except this time it showed a new cast of characters.

"Is that...?" I trailed off, unsure if I was correct.

"Ruad, yes."

I looked more closely then, examining the monstrous figure as he donned armor and trained in a courtyard. A beautiful dark-haired woman could be seen beyond, observing the goings-on and him intently.

The image changed, and they were holding a

newborn baby, the love between them palpable. Then, the child as he grew, his features so similar to his father's.

The crystal swirled black then, and a funeral filled the sphere. Ruad and the woman were there, but the son was not. Looking closer at the likeness on the sarcophagus, I gasped.

When I whipped my head to look at Amergin, he smiled sadly but indicated I should continue watching. I did as he asked, and the scenes grew more horrific. I could see the woman mourning, wailing, her grief tearing her apart. Then her own coffin and Ruad standing sentry long after the rest of the mourners were gone.

The rest was a bit of a blur, the images flashing faster, but the pair were in them as well. Ruad and the woman in different manners of dress, with altered hairstyles and backgrounds. Finally, it showed the woman with a red-haired man, but this time Ruad wasn't there. The crystal went translucent once more, becoming a stone again.

"What was that?" I asked, tears welling despite myself.

"The love of Ruad's life, Brigid."

"Wait." There was one Brigid we all knew. "Not Dagda's daughter?"

"One and the same," he said.

"But she... didn't she... how can she...?" I trailed off, not sure if my facts were accurate. Though I had seen it myself. She was no longer with us.

"She was, yes. That's what we're up against. The queen is raising an army to overthrow Dagda, and she will stop at nothing to do it. Brigid is, and has always been, a bartering tool in this war to overthrow him. The queen has brought her back to try to manipulate Ruad, his greatest weakness."

"But I don't understand."

"As he is Dagda's most trusted adviser and most feared weapon, she hopes to disarm Ruad first in her coup. That's why he was here, to temper his hopes."

"Hopes?"

"That he could have her finally, this would be the end of this cycle, and he could end her suffering."

"This cycle? Can he?"

"As you learn more, you'll see there're different cycles all playing out at the same time but at different stages and in different ways. Sometimes with the same people, other times with all new players. Brigid and Ruad have been playing this cycle out for millennia. It's not the first game they have been a part of, and, well, it may be the last.

But it still doesn't mean Ruad gets his girl at the end."

I sat there for a moment, wrapping my head around the information.

"But if this is the end of the cycle, what do we have to do?"

"Everything! If this is the end, it means we do something. We make a difference. Somehow, we end this farce—at least for now."

"For now?"

"It doesn't mean it won't crop up again, but what that vision told me is that at least we changed something. If Ruad is no longer in the cycle, it's because it's changing, and whatever new one takes its place won't be the same as before. And whether it's for the better or worse, we won't know until we're there. Or, rather, our predecessors get there.

"It's history, doomed to repeat until we learn the lesson and move on. By this alternative ending, perhaps we, humanity, have finally learned enough that we no longer need to repeat the same old story. Does that make sense? We have evolved beyond it, or that's the goal, at least."

When he said it that way, it made more sense. I still was failing to understand what role I played in it, though.

"So, how do we end it?"

"That's the question. One we'll discover together, I suspect."

"Well, I can't wait," I said without enthusiasm. "We can't figure out a way for Ruad and Brigid to be together?"

"Ah, I would if I could. Ruad's heartache is near and dear to me, but we can't write what's not written. We're only the ministers of the word, not the authors. Ruad comes to me often for what the Fates tell me, and I've never had good news for him. Though I think today's report was more favorable to him. He cares less for his own happiness than for hers. I think she's finally going to have it."

"Without him, though?"

"Perhaps with him with any luck. But by what is written that I've been able to read, no."

"That's... horrible," I said, and I meant it. Knowing a bit of their story, it made my heart hurt physically. I rubbed at the ache to ease the discomfort.

"Worse, honey. It's despicable. But if you haven't already noticed, we don't have the full picture. I don't know what him not being with her at the end means, nor do I get the full set of instructions on how to accomplish whatever we're going to do. It's a lot more knowing what to ask and when to listen, how to pay attention to the signs around you."

"Does that mean they can end up together?"

"I think there's a chance, more of one than there's ever been. And it's equally possible that Ruad is permanently out of the picture, and Brigid will have no choice but to move on."

"She couldn't possibly," I said, a little upset at the idea. A love like that, no one could move on from.

He shook his head.

"When Brigid is *brought back*," he said, trying to find the words for it, "she doesn't remember anything. Sometimes she'll start to remember; other times Ruad helps her. And every now and again, she's not around long enough for it to matter. If she moves on, believe me, Ruad is only happy that it can be over for her, for both of them."

"But why can't they be together?"

"Brigid is Dagda's daughter. She has a political sway. Her hand was always sworn to Bres, to unite the Tuatha de Danann with the Fomorians. Her father would never let her be with Ruad—his most trusted adviser and warrior, sure, but not royal blood and not a prosperous marriage for her.

"Heaven knows how much we have all tried to

change that, but it's never worked. Dagda may be fair by most accounts, but he rules with an iron fist. Perhaps in another lifetime, they can be together. For now, I don't foretell that happening."

"It's so miserable, though."

"Honey, there is no end to the misery this cycle brings. But if we can end it, and I pray we will, then more than just Ruad will be grateful for it."

I thought of all the suffering I'd been dealt, not only the death of my parents but so many injustices before then. Ruad and Brigid's star-crossed love story, Amergin losing his wife, and all the Druids who had to hide and suffer in silence—never mind the towns and farms we had passed with nothing but ashes and bones left.

Shaking out the vestiges of my fears, I looked at Amergin.

"Well, let's do it, then."

CHAPTER

# THIRTEEN

W<small>E WOKE UP BRIGHT AND EARLY THE NEXT MORNING AND</small> did our morning rituals in silence before heading to forage for more herbs. The day was cold, and the wind whipped my hair and stung my face. I was thinking I wasn't quite ready to save the world anymore, relinquishing the plan in favor of curling up under the covers again.

Something wasn't right, though. The woods were silent in a way that had me looking at Amergin with a suspicion reflected in his gaze. He grabbed my arm to pull me closer and behind him as we crept silently along the edge of the tree line.

I hovered close to him with my head on a swivel, but nothing caught my eye. Amergin cursed, and I looked to see him bleeding from his temple, though I didn't remember hearing a sound.

Up ahead, two figures came out into the clearing, and I squinted to see them better, curling further behind Amergin even as he pushed me there. It was a little weak, but I hadn't a clue what was happening, and he didn't seem too injured to play hero yet.

They looked familiar, and it took a while to place them, but finally, I did. It was only when white hair came peeking around the corner, mouth bound with a cloth and hands tied in front of her, that I recognized them as the men from the kitchen that day ages ago.

Evelyn looked a little worse for wear, but she was in one piece and didn't seem harmed. But I'd never seen a hair out of place on her head in my life, and now it stuck out at odd angles and was in need of a trim.

I stepped out from behind Amergin then, much to his dismay, but I wouldn't back down this time. Not when their man had tried hustling us the first time, and certainly not when my Evelyn was in their hands.

"What the fuck is wrong with you?" I spat, anger bursting forth, a volcano spewing magma.

"Trade places, darling, and we might tell you," the taller one taunted, smirking suggestively.

It made me want to vomit, but I held my tongue, trying to play this through in my head. Amergin had gone rigid as a stone beside me, but he kept an arm over my middle to keep me from going much closer.

"Let her go," I said with venom.

Rage became a wild thing inside me, spiking my heart rate and making me gasp for breath. Everything was sharpened, fear and anger giving this a stark relief as I pinpointed the focus of my ire.

Rocks rumbled around us, and it broke my concentration if only slightly, but then suddenly, they stopped. The man closer to Evelyn, the shorter one, grabbed her, and I couldn't see as much as hear the clattering starting up again.

"Come here, and I'll cut her free," he said, and I glimpsed the knife glinting at his side.

There was never a question of when I would go with them, only how. Hostage negotiation was not something Amergin had covered in his teachings, but listening to my inner voice was.

"Cut her free first, and I'll go," I said.

"Emer, don't," Amergin said beside me, the first words he'd spoken.

I wanted to elbow him in the ribs for his stupid

rigidity, to tear him apart for his stoicism. Couldn't he see poor Evelyn, defenseless and scared? Where was his audacity now? Wasn't he the one to fear, not me?

Instead, the short man held the knife to her throat, and I stopped breathing. A flash of white caught my eye behind them, and I nearly cried in relief.

Whalen.

"You don't make demands of us. Now get over here before I slit her throat and make you watch the way you did to us," the man seethed.

I didn't have a lot of time to deliberate as I watched him apply pressure to her neck. Her eyes were scared but not mad. If anything, there was acceptance in her gaze as well as forgiveness.

Gods help me but this woman was giving me peace even now. As if she could bear this horrible death but not me haranguing myself for eternity over it.

My body couldn't contain the rage that exploded inside me. Adrenaline pumped wildly, numbing my fingers, my face, and my fear. Paralyzing everything but the urge to move.

I took a step forward, and Amergin pulled me back again. This time I growled as I swatted his hand away. He could fuck right off if he thought I would let him stop me.

But how to stall?

"Remember to focus," Amergin said quietly as I broached the gap.

*Focus on what? Your inability to protect this harmless old woman? Or is it unwillingness?*

I snapped a vicious glare his way, but he didn't seem shaken or discomfited. He may have even smiled.

That's when Amergin's words surfaced through the haze of emotions. *Focus on what could go right, what is going well right now.*

Replacing images of Evelyn's lifeless body on the ground as her blood gushed from a severed artery in her neck with ones of her embracing me after this ordeal helped. I imagined him releasing her to Amergin as I got close enough to wield my own dagger and plunged it into the tall one's belly as Whalen tore the other's throat.

Strangely, I felt better, less out of control... if killing people could make anyone feel calm.

About halfway across was when I paused my advance, leaning into the feeling of how I wanted things to go.

"Now let her go, unharmed. Hand her to him," I said, nodding toward Amergin's still figure.

I expected more backlash, but he removed the knife from her neck. As he walked her forward, I took another step toward his awaiting companion until we were in tempo. Step after step, we inched closer to opposite goals.

Until he stuck the knife in Evelyn's back before shoving her the last foot toward Amergin. I screamed in horror as she hit the ground, unsettled by his push and the wound.

Red seeped through her dress, but I had hardly a moment to assess the damage before the tall guy yanked me violently toward him by my hair. This, however, I was ready for.

The blade was warm in my cold hands, blood pooling in my core and away from my extremities in my distress. But his blood was like fire.

He didn't prepare for that eventuality, it seemed, as he gasped and looked at me with a fury I had never seen before. Pain bloomed in my head as he reeled a hand into my jaw, the impact knocking me off my feet.

My hair still remained in his grip, and I prepared for a second impact as he pulled his free arm back to slam into my face again. Striking out with the knife,

I knew I made contact as he shouted, and the next hit never came. But in the fray, I had lost my knife.

It seemed he lost his grip on my hair, too, and I didn't waste the chance. Grabbing a rock out of thin air, I hurled it at his face, hitting my mark in a sickening thud. After throwing a handful of dirt into his eyes, I was on my feet, kicking him square in the face, the ribs, the kidneys.

I kept kicking and screaming, and a flash of white blew past me. The man on the ground was immobile, so I dared a look toward the White Wolf as he quickly dispatched the short man. A sick satisfaction whirled through me when he was lifeless.

But the wolf didn't stop there. Hurtling over the fallen man's body, he dove for Amergin next. Joseph was kneeling beside Evelyn. How or when he got there, I didn't know, but he had her head propped up on his bag and had removed his shirt to use it as a makeshift bandage.

Oisin flashed through my mind, bandaged and battered in the cellar of the barn. Joseph had patched him up, too, and he was fine now.

I tore my eyes from them to focus on the battle between Amergin and Whalen. The White Wolf's wrath was something to behold as his fangs glistened red with blood, his hackles raised as he growled at Amergin.

"Whalen!" I shouted, running in between.

Joseph cut me off, quick as lightning. The look on his face was glacial.

"He's earned it," he said, and then he was gone, back to Evelyn with his kit out.

He had taken off the gag and handcuffs, and she lay there, looking fragile but determined as she gritted her teeth against the pain. Joseph lowered his head to her back, fangs out.

"Joseph!" I shouted then, racing to stop him now.

Skin squelched softly under his fangs. Grabbing his shoulders, I pulled with all my might, but he didn't move an inch.

Evelyn's soft voice came from the other side of him. "It coagulates the blood, dear."

A sob escaped my throat. Skidding to the ground near her head, I laid my forehead against her temple, the most I could allow myself.

"It'll be all right, dear. This old body hasn't failed me yet," she said, patting my hair with the hand nearest the ground.

She winced, though, and it radiated through the

shrug of muscles. Grabbing her hand, I held it in mine, back on the ground to keep her still.

Snarls and growls rent the air, bringing my attention back to the battle being waged between the wolf and the Druid. For all of Whalen's lunges, though, Amergin parried with grace, as if he knew the movements before they were made. The frustration only made the wolf more irate at being blocked with invisible barriers or hit with unseen blows.

Amergin's hands moved with deftness and precision, but he never physically touched Whalen, not that I could see. As he whirled spells left and right, though, he spoke.

"Did you think I would so soon forget your insolence?" he demanded, flicking his wrist so a volley of rocks flew into Whalen's flank.

The wolf didn't wince, though, only bore down and bared his teeth. Chills raced down my spine to witness the legend himself in action, or as close as I'd seen yet.

Amergin was staring the beast in his eyes, the wolf's massive shoulders hunched as he stalked his prey. He kept taunting him, though, with more hand movements that made Whalen twitch but never wince in pain.

I thought it was either incredibly bold or

massively stupid on Amergin's part to goad him that way. Perhaps both.

"My wife. You were meant to protect her, and you abandoned her in your selfishness and your *stupidity*, and then you come here as if nothing has happened and ask for a favor?" He threw another volley of detritus, a wave of power so strong, it brought the wolf to his knees.

"What is he saying?" I asked Joseph, alarm bells clanging in my head, but Amergin's voice boomed again.

He screamed louder, the deep timbre of his voice echoing against the trees. "She *died* because of *you*, and I've spent centuries mourning her. I expect to see her around every corner, in bed when I wake. Every bright thing in my life has been robbed of joy because of *you*!"

The ground began rumbling as Amergin held his hands out toward Whalen.

What did he mean, his wife was dead because of him? What did Whalen do?

Images whirled in my head again: my parents, whose deaths I couldn't properly mourn because I couldn't claim them as mine. Forbidden the chance to bury them, to reconcile the child I had been with the woman I was becoming. I would never see their faces again or hold them close.

Suddenly I was filled with as much rage as Amergin. Was Whalen responsible for their deaths and lied about it?

The wolf made a sound to shatter the earth as he broke through whatever spell had been restraining him. Lunging, he tackled the Druid to the ground, and Amergin's head hit with a thud.

Invisible blows landed, and the wolf winced and trembled before he lost his footing, and the pair tumbled in a dizzying dance of attacks. A swipe of one monstrous paw tore through Amergin's abdomen, and a rock shattered against Whalen's temple. Blood flowed freely, mixing with the other's and the dirt below them.

"That's not true, is it?" I whispered to Joseph above the noise.

He didn't say anything or acknowledge I had even spoken. Instead, his dark eyes were focused wholly on the brawl in front of us, which was an answer in itself.

Amergin landed a blow to the wolf's belly that made him reel enough to give the Druid some breathing room. They both panted wildly, but it didn't stop Amergin from smiling before he spoke.

"You didn't tell her, did you?"

Whalen growled low and menacing as he stretched out his wounded abdomen. Both men had paused long enough to catch their breath, though maybe Amergin had planned it this way.

"Did you fail to mention that those men, the ones who slaughtered the people she knew and loved, could have been stopped? That you had them in your sights, but you were biding your time, waiting for them to lead you to the queen, to me?"

The words took a second to sink in, to penetrate my mind and create a picture for me. Whalen could have stopped them but chose not to.

I carefully watched his expression as the words hung heavy in the silence between us. I didn't appreciate what I saw.

"You *liar!*" I screamed, throwing a spell of my own at Whalen.

I didn't know whether the force or the shock got him, but it dropped him to the ground. Evelyn grabbed at me to stop my progress, but I couldn't be swayed, not even by her.

Forgoing my training for sheer savagery, I picked up rocks and hurtled them at Whalen with abandon. They hit their mark—each and every one of them.

Hurling all my rage and despair at him, I didn't

stop until exhaustion finally crept in. Amergin had pulled away from Whalen completely, forgotten in the melee.

Whalen stood in front of me in wolf form, his yellow eyes guarded. My chest heaved with spent adrenaline, my limbs oddly numb.

Evelyn called behind me, her voice too quiet for me to hear, perhaps alarmingly so. I wasn't sure anything she said would have made a difference, though.

If Amergin spoke true and Whalen was responsible for him losing his wife—if he truly didn't stop those men from attacking my clan—I was at a loss.

Outrage warred with emotions I still chose not to accept. I wanted to hit him and kick him and scream until my voice was gone and my limbs couldn't move anymore. But looking at the pain and sorrow reflected in his gaze held me still.

Beating the hell out of Whalen wasn't going to solve anything, I knew. And torturing him more than he was already doing to himself lacked appeal. I did, however, despise his face right now.

"Get the fuck away from me," I said, my voice harsh and cold.

He couldn't respond, not in his wolf form, but

his eyes said it all. They pleaded with me, but I had no sympathy in my bones for him right then.

"Now" was all I said.

My body still vibrated with unspent rage, but he didn't argue further, nor did he say a farewell. With a final glare at Amergin and a glance at Joseph, he turned and went.

A strange part of me wished he had at least said goodbye.

---

Book two will be released in 2025.

# ACKNOWLEDGMENTS

Who should I thank first? That is the question. I will write a second novel's worth if I name individual family members. Succinctly, my grandmother inspired my love of books, my parents bought them, and my siblings recommended new ones. To the family I chose, I'll never be able to explain how grateful I am to you all. For my husband's unconditional love and support, and my children for the same love and then some, you are the half that made me whole.

My dear friend, who shall remain nameless, I want to express my deepest gratitude for everything you have done for me. I cannot fathom how the universe orchestrated our meeting, but I am certain that without you, I wouldn't be composing these words. Encountering you has given me a true understanding of the power of manifestation. It's about being in the right place at the right time, putting in the effort, and allowing the universe to conspire in your favor. After all, you'll never know unless you try.

Last but not least, I want to express my gratitude to the amazing staff at Hot Tree Publishing. You all made me feel at home instantly. Thank you for taking a chance on me, encouraging me, and helping me fix my numerous mistakes. There were so many missing and added commas.

Dear reader, thank you for giving me a chance. I'll never be able to explain that feeling, but what you do makes a difference, even if you don't always see it. If you're ever reaching for something more, keep your eyes peeled for the signs. They are there if you pay attention. But most importantly, keep putting one foot in front of the other, and count your blessings. If nothing is guaranteed, then everything is a gift. Thank you for your gift of supporting me.

# About the Author

Shea was born and raised in New Jersey in an Irish and Italian family. She usually sits with a book in her hands and two more in her bag for backup. Pursuing education and psychology in college, she always wanted to make a difference in the world. A lifelong learner and travel enthusiast, she combined her passions in her writing, where fantasy, history, and romance abound. Her writing highlights mental health topics in a relatable way, where the underdog never fails to surprise, usually with a handsome man or two, sarcasm, and folklore. She resides with her husband and children, writing her love story daily.

facebook.com/sheahulse

instagram.com/sheahulse13

tiktok.com/@sheahulse

bookbub.com/authors/shea-hulse

# ABOUT THE PUBLISHER

**Hot Tree Publishing loves love.** Publishing adult romantic fiction, HTPubs are all about diverse reads featuring heroes and heroines to swoon over. Since opening in 2015, HTPubs have published more than 300 titles across the wide and diverse range of romantic genres. If you're chasing a happily ever after in your favourite subgenre, HTPubs have you covered.

Interested in discovering more amazing reads brought to you by Hot Tree Publishing? Head over to the website for information:

WWW.HOTTREEPUBLISHING.COM

facebook.com/hottreepublishing

x.com/hottreepubs

instagram.com/hottreepublishing

tiktok.com/@hottreepublishing